EVERS & AFTERS

A Dare With Me Novel

J.H. CROIX

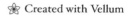 Created with Vellum

DEDICATION

To my friends who remind me time and again it's about how to take care of each other. Sometimes that means wine and chocolate over videoconference.

Sign up for my newsletter for information on new releases & get a FREE copy of one of my books!

http://jhcroixauthor.com/subscribe/

Follow me!
  jhcroix@jhcroix.com
  https://amazon.com/author/jhcroix
  https://www.bookbub.com/authors/j-h-croix
  https://www.facebook.com/jhcroix
  https://www.instagram.com/jhcroix/

Chapter One

ELIAS

November

"You have a visitor, Elias," the nurse said in a cheerful voice.

I resisted the urge to actually growl at her and managed a tight smile in return. "I wasn't expecting anyone," I replied.

"Well, the coffee around here isn't the best, so I think you'll appreciate this visitor."

I didn't know this nurse's name. She wasn't one of the regulars. I'd only been here three days, and I'd already figured out the usual staff.

I closed my eyes and leaned my head against my pillows. Being in the hospital sucked. My throbbing side annoyed me, and I wanted to be out of here yesterday. Now, I had a freaking visitor. I only hoped it was someone I liked enough that they wouldn't mind me being an asshole.

"Elias?" a voice called softly.

I ransacked my brain for a moment because I knew

that voice. My weary, achy body gave itself a shake. Then, I spied her. It was Cammi Taylor. Opening my eyes, I saw her step into my hospital room and close the door behind her. She had a cup of coffee in her hands, and my mouth almost started watering because Cammi made the best damn coffee in town. Hell, in all of Alaska as far as I was concerned. Considering that I flew all over the state and visited many coffee shops, including the high-end ones in a few cities, my opinion was based on strong research.

She turned, her blue eyes lighting up when she saw me awake. "Hey," she said as she crossed the room. "I brought you some coffee."

I sat up a little straighter in bed and silently cursed the effect Cammi had on me. Every cell in my body sat up and took notice when she was nearby. I'd been getting coffee at her coffee shop for five years now. Red Truck Coffee was impossible to miss when you drove past it on the way to the airport. It was in an old red baker's truck, a beacon representing incredible coffee and Cammi's warm smile. I started going there for the coffee, and now I couldn't be sure it wasn't Cammi that drew me in like a magnet. Every time I saw her, I had to beat back my body's intense reaction.

When I first met her, her hair was short, but she'd let it grow out and it fell in a silky bob, swinging forward as she sat down in the chair beside my bed and held up the distinctive red paper coffee cup. "Here you go."

I ignored the twinge of pain as I lifted my hand to reach for the coffee. I took a swallow, letting out a low groan at the decadent and rich flavor.

Opening my eyes, I met hers, my lips tugging into an unbidden smile. "Thank you. The coffee here is shit."

Cammi's laugh was like soft bells in the room, and I felt a tug low in my chest. "I'm sure they do the best they can, but their priorities are taking care of their patients. How are you feeling?" Her concerned eyes coasted over me.

I felt like hell, but I didn't want to complain. I hated how weak and useless I felt in the hospital.

I lifted my shoulder in a shrug. "Okay. Better now that you brought me this." I took another healthy swallow.

I tried to adjust the pillows behind me and swore when I couldn't get it right. Next thing I knew, Cammi was standing beside the bed fussing over me.

"Elias, take it easy. Here," she murmured. She leaned over me, adjusting the pillows behind my back.

I closed my eyes, taking a breath, and instantly getting a hit of Cammi—she smelled like sugar, coffee and sweetness. Jesus, this girl made me crazy.

I hated how helpless I felt, laid up in a hospital bed. I'd been arguing with the doctor about my discharge ever since I woke up here.

I was both relieved and disappointed when she moved away. Of course, she got the pillows just right so I was more comfortable.

She straightened, her face inches from mine when she asked, "Better?"

The air around us felt lit with a charge. Her blue eyes had layers of color in them, like the ocean under the sun. My eyes landed on her rosebud mouth. There I was, laid up in a hospital bed, cranky and probably acting like an asshole, and I was a hair's breadth away from kissing her.

I didn't realize I hadn't even replied to her until I saw a flush cresting on her cheeks. "Elias?" she prompted.

Oh, right. I was too busy staring at her mouth. I brought my eyes back to hers and cleared my throat, my answer coming out rough. "Definitely better. Thank you."

Cammi sat back down. "I'll bring you coffee tomorrow too. Actually, are you getting out before tomorrow?"

I reached for the cup of coffee again, this time able to reach it easily on the table beside my bed. I needed another sip of Cammi's fine elixir. After a long swallow, I lowered the cup and let out a sigh. "I don't know."

"Well, you don't want to get out before they think you're ready," she said matter-of-factly.

"I'm ready," I insisted.

Her lips twitched, and I felt my own laugh bubbling up. I didn't want to admit it, but I knew she was right. When I finally did let a laugh loose, I followed it with a shuddering breath because it made my side hurt.

"Oh!" She pressed her hand to her heart. "I'm sorry. I didn't mean to make you laugh."

She looked so genuinely worried that I felt pressed to reassure her. "You didn't make me laugh. I'm laughing at myself. I'm just impatient to get out of here. Rumor has it I might get discharged tomorrow afternoon."

"Then, I'll definitely bring you coffee in the morning. It'll cheer you up before it's time to go." Worry suddenly crossed her features, a crease forming between her brows. "Wait a sec, are you even supposed to drink coffee? The nurse knew I had it, but maybe she thought it was mine."

Cammi started to stand from her chair, and I thought she was actually going to call the freaking nurse to my room.

"I'm allowed to have coffee," I said. "Please sit down."

She sat down quickly. "Are you sure?"

"Sure about what?"

Right then, the doctor, who looked young enough to be straight out of college, came through the door, his eyes flicking between Cammi and me. "Glad to see you're having visitors," he commented as he walked in.

I felt the scowl form on my face. I'd been perpetually annoyed ever since I'd landed here after the accident. I'd had a minor plane crash with my friend a few days before. He'd skated out with fewer injuries then me. I had a nasty ankle break and a doozy of a gash in one side from a piece of metal. I still thought they should've discharged me once surgery was over.

Cammi, of course, smiled. She was nicer than me. "Hi there. How is Elias doing?"

"We should be able to clear him for discharge tomorrow, assuming the checkup we do tomorrow looks good." The doctor gave me a critical look. He stopped at the foot of my bed, tapping on the small computer tablet that seemed to be permanently in his hands.

When I glanced toward Cammi again—because I couldn't freaking help it—I got that usual sweet shot when my eyes collided with hers. It seemed there was nothing I could do about that.

She smiled encouragingly. "That's great. Is he taking enough medication for his pain? Because he doesn't seem very comfortable."

I practically growled at her. "I'm fine. I do *not* need anything else for my pain."

Cammi didn't need to know that I'd once come way too close to getting hooked on painkillers. I'd faced what felt like an endless desert of pain after the accident that killed a friend and landed me facing the end of my career as a pilot in the Air Force. Unrelenting with no end in sight, opiate painkillers had felt like manna from heaven, a relief from the pain and an escape from the thoughts chasing in circles in my mind.

Although the doctor here drove me kind of nuts, he seemed to understand my resistance to medication and didn't push it.

"He's hanging in there. Maybe he's a little cranky," the doctor said with a quick grin in my direction, "but not many people love the hospital. It's nice to know he's got a girlfriend who cares about him."

I almost choked. Cammi's pretty blue eyes widened slightly with a wash of pink cresting on her cheeks. She opened her mouth to reply right as his pager buzzed in the room. "I'll be back to check in later."

Just like that, he was gone. "I'll make sure to clarify you're not my girlfriend," I muttered.

Cammi shrugged lightly, her eyes coasting over my face. I hated feeling weak, I hated being in pain, and I hated that all of that was obvious to anyone who saw me. Even worse, Cammi tended to make me feel as if she could see right through me, and it drove me crazy.

"It's a harmless misunderstanding. By all means, make sure to correct him though." Her lips twisted to the side. She actually looked a little hurt, and I felt a twinge of guilt.

"Cammi, that's not it. I'm an ass and definitely not at my best in here. For that I'm sorry," I said sincerely.

Chapter Two

CAMMI

Elias actually looked like he felt bad. Good Lord, this man was dangerous for my sanity. There he sat in a hospital bed with the sheet draped at his hips, and his hospital gown barely concealing his chest and doing a whole lot of nothing to hide the lean muscles of his arms and shoulders.

His shaggy dark blond hair was rumpled, falling almost to his shoulders on the sides. His piercing espresso eyes met mine. I took a moment to study him. His skin was burnished bronze, even in the middle of winter. Being alone near him had my libido giving itself a shake and perking up like a cheerful puppy after a nap. It did that every time I saw Elias.

His face was a thing of beauty—cut cheekbones, and a strong jaw with a little dimple at the bottom of his chin. His rich brown eyes stood out, and oh my word, his lips were bold and sensual. Just looking at him made my mouth water a little. Being in the hospital, his raw masculinity should've been a little weaker now. I mean, he *was* injured. I tried to convince my body to cool its heels, but no such luck.

Of course, being Elias, the reason for him being in the hospital was no mundane accident. Oh no, even that carried an edge of sexy danger. He and his friend crashed in the wilderness in a small plane. Elias had braved cold weather and stayed conscious the entire time with cracked ribs, a broken ankle, and a nasty gash on his side, according to my friend who had given me the scoop.

Injured and in a hospital bed, Elias *still* had that crazy effect on me. Every time I looked at him, it was like getting a hit of hotness. My hormones lit up like a pinball machine, and my libido did a little dance. As far as I could tell, it was a one-way street.

I hadn't come to the hospital with designs on Elias. I'd gotten to know him over the last few years when he stopped by for coffee almost daily at my little coffee truck. Even though he was usually a grumpy guy, he was a very reliable customer and left ridiculous tips, like five bucks for a three-dollar coffee. Even if he didn't call himself my friend, I considered him part of my circle, such as it was in the small world of Diamond Creek, Alaska.

"It's okay, I know I'm not your girlfriend. I wasn't confused about that part," I teased, injecting lightness into my tone.

"I know you're not," he said, his voice coming out a little rough. "I hate being here, and it makes me more of an ass than usual."

"You're not an ass, and you'll be free tomorrow," I said, my heart squeezing a little. He looked like a lost boy. "Like I said, I'll bring coffee tomorrow for you. It'll improve your morning."

"That'd be more than nice. How are things?"

"Be careful now," I teased. "We're about to have the longest conversation we've ever had."

Elias stared back at me, just long enough that I wondered if I saw heat flicker in his eyes. Surely not. Because that was crazy thinking.

Just then, the door to his room opened again, and Flynn Walker came striding in. Flynn was another gorgeous specimen of a man, tall and lanky with dark blond hair, and glacial blue eyes. There were plenty of women who pined after him.

He was a lost cause, or so I kept telling every girl who'd listen. He was beyond in love with Daphne Bell who was the chef at the outdoor resort he ran on the outskirts of Diamond Creek. I was thrilled for them.

Flynn flew planes with Elias and rumor had it they'd been in the Air Force together, along with the rest of the pilots who worked for Flynn. Flynn wore battered jeans and a navy T-shirt that made his eyes pop. He stopped beside the bed, looking from me to Elias. "Is he being nice to you?" he asked with a sly grin.

"Absolutely," I said sweetly.

"I was only a little cranky," Elias added. "I even let the doctor think she's my girlfriend."

Flynn's eyes went comically wide at that. "Damn. I guess that means she *is* your girlfriend."

Elias actually laughed, and then immediately grimaced.

"Take it easy," Flynn said.

"It's my fucking ribs, man."

"I feel you," Flynn replied, patting his own side. "You know I cracked a few. I'm still sore."

"Yeah, but you're not in the fucking hospital," Elias muttered.

"Dude, it's only been three days," Flynn said.

"Yeah, but you're free. You didn't have to spend the night," Elias argued.

"Yeah, well, I didn't get stabbed in the side with a branch and a piece of metal. You did."

Elias rolled his eyes with a sigh. "I'm gonna have a hell of a scar."

"Well, scars are badass. Right, Cammi?" Flynn glanced toward me.

"I prefer for my friends to *not* almost die," I said sincerely.

"Let me see that side anyway," Flynn commented, stepping closer to the bed.

A wash of heat blasted through me when Elias slid one arm out of his hospital gown and bared his chest and abdomen. I'd never actually seen him without a shirt. Now, I knew for sure he had a genuine six-pack, maybe even an eight-pack. My fingers twitched. Oh my God. I was getting hot and bothered over a guy in a hospital bed.

Elias pushed the fabric over further, and I gasped. He had a wound, probably eight inches long on his side, about halfway between his waist and armpit. There was a tidy line of stitches and it appeared to be healing nicely. I didn't like thinking about what it must have looked like before it was stitched up. The entire area surrounding it was still bruised.

Flynn whistled through his teeth. "Ouch. The bruising is ugly, so that means the swelling is going down. You're well on your way," he offered encouragingly, unperturbed at the sight of Elias's injury. "So, it's that and your broken ankle, right?"

Elias nodded. "Yup. They had to repair my spleen where it got nicked and put a pin in my ankle."

My heart twisted in my chest, and I wanted to take Elias home, wrap him in a warm comforter and ply him with tea and coffee and sweets. My response to Elias made me feel a little crazy. It alternated between pure lust and this sudden desire to take care of him. As if Elias needed anyone to take care of him.

"What time is your get out of jail card scheduled for tomorrow?" Flynn's question drew me back into the conversation.

"The doctor said in the afternoon. They have to clear me before they truly agree to set me free."

"I'm bringing him coffee in the morning so he'll be in a better mood," I offered.

Flynn chuckled. "Daphne is making him something special for dinner. You'll get spoiled when you come home."

"I'll stay out in the other house," Elias muttered.

"No can-do," Flynn said. "A nurse called this morning to make sure somebody could help when you change the dressing on that injury, and you still can't get around on that leg. Daphne's gonna set you up downstairs. It's a win-win."

"Okay, I know you're crazy about Daphne, and I think she's awesome, but how do I win?"

"You get a bed downstairs and amazing food, plus all your friends get to visit."

My phone rang, and I slipped it out of my purse, glancing down to see my friend Susie's name flash on the screen. I stood and glanced between them. "I should get going. I'll see you tomorrow morning," I said, casting a last smile at Elias.

Chapter Three

ELIAS

"Why?" Daphne demanded.

"Because I don't need it," I muttered, trying to keep the frustration out of my tone.

At that moment, Flynn came walking in the room. His gaze arced from me to Daphne. "Babe, I know you want him to take more pain medication, but he's not going for it."

Flynn's girlfriend let out a little huff of frustration. "Fine. Then, I'll make your favorite muffins."

My lips tugged into a reluctant smile. "Food will definitely improve my mood, especially anything you make."

She gave me a worried smile. Crossing over to my bed, she pointlessly adjusted the pillows behind me. "Are you sure your leg is comfortable?" she asked as she straightened.

I looked up at Daphne, who had stolen Flynn's heart so neatly and completely, I think he was still occasionally shocked by it. He called her princess, because she looked like one. Or, rather, she had the vibe. With auburn hair and stunning green eyes, she had a petite build, and even when she was dressed casually, she looked perfectly put together. She was a shockingly good cook and had made our lives here even better, just because she spoiled us like crazy. Ending up with a chef who could probably have a hit restaurant in any city out here in the middle of almost nowhere Alaska was pretty freaking awesome.

"My leg is fine," I replied. Because it was. My ankle was achy, but that was to be expected.

She gave me another smile. "All right. I'll be back in a bit."

Daphne turned and hurried away, leaving me alone with Flynn. Flynn Walker was one of my best friends and also technically my boss. He sat down in the chair Daphne, ever helpful, had situated beside my bed. His eyes flicked down toward my ankle, which was in a fucking cast. He ran a hand through his hair as he leaned back in the chair.

Flynn and I had served in the Air Force together. Aside from Flynn's brother, and his sister, Nora, who was finishing her flight training hours, the rest of us had met during our time in the Air Force. Flynn had left the Air Force two years before me to come home and take care of his younger siblings after their mother died. Flynn's father disappeared long ago, and his step-father, father to the rest of his siblings, had passed away a few years earlier. In a way, Flynn was the father his siblings never had. He'd pulled everything together and gotten this outdoor resort up and running.

Working here was a dream job for me. I got to fly planes all the time, and flying planes in Alaska was pretty sweet. The view was incredible no matter where you were.

Flynn's sharp gaze made its way back to my face. "Are you okay?"

I lifted a shoulder in a light shrug. "Define okay."

He chuckled. "Dude, I know it sucks. You'll be on your feet soon. How is the pain? Really."

"Tolerable."

Flynn was one of the few people who knew about my prior brush with getting a little too comfortable with painkillers. I didn't want any. I would just live with the pain rather than tempt my body back to that place.

While those pills could work magic for pain, they hijacked your brain. I'd take pain any day over that feeling of standing on the edge of desperation.

"It would help if you mentioned to Daphne why you don't want to take any meds. She won't bug you about it then," he offered.

I leaned back in the pillows, letting out a ragged sigh. "Dude, I know you love her, but I fucking hate talking about that shit."

"I don't want you to tell her because I love her. She gets it. She's been through her own version of hell, and she won't judge you. But maybe if she knows, she won't nag you."

"I'll think about it."

"What did the doctor say about how long you'll need that cast?" he asked, kind enough to change the subject.

"He said six to eight weeks. I'll be ready to fly before you know it," I replied.

"You're not flying anywhere until you have medical clearance," Flynn said, just as Diego came in the room.

Diego Jackson was another friend from the Air Force. Like me, when Flynn gave him the chance to fly planes for a living in God's country, he jumped at it.

Diego chuckled, his eyes flashing as he divided his gaze between Flynn and me. "Flynn's gonna be strict about that. You can be my copilot anytime, even with a cast on."

Flynn cast him a glare. "Dude, don't pull that shit."

Diego stopped beside the bed as he cuffed Flynn lightly on the shoulder. "Just fucking with you. Daphne's making your favorite muffins. She says they'll be ready in an hour."

Flynn stood from his chair, stepping back. Gesturing to it, he commented, "Why don't you keep cranky here company? I was just coming in to check in and let you know I'll be in town today. You need anything?"

"I can't do anything, so what would I need?" I returned.

Diego hooked his hand on the back of the chair, turning it to face toward the windows as he sat down. "You can do stuff. You just gotta walk on your crutches."

I rolled my eyes. Flynn turned and began walking out of the room, pausing by the door. "Text me if you think of anything. I'll stop by the grocery store before I come back."

"Make sure to get some beer," Diego called.

"I don't need to be reminded of that," Flynn replied as he lifted his hand in a wave and then left the room.

Diego's eyes scanned the space before coming back to me. "Daphne fixed this room up nice for you."

They'd put me up in the only guest room in the downstairs of the resort. When Daphne came to stay, she had originally been an actual guest and stayed upstairs where guest rooms occupied to the two upper floors. Then, she stayed on after Flynn chased away another cook and moved down here before she and Flynn finally fessed up to being in love with each other. Despite my irritation with the situation, I was in a ridiculously comfortable bed with a fluffy down quilt and enough pillows for about five people.

"Of course, she did. It was spotless already."

Diego's green gaze landed on mine. "It looks like she gave you some extra pillows," he observed. "If you don't need them all, I'll take a few."

I lifted a pillow with my good arm and tossed it toward him. He caught it easily with a chuckle. "I'm glad you're okay, man," he said, his gaze sobering.

"Thanks. I'm okay enough to be annoyed while I recover. It's boring."

Diego was quiet as he regarded me. "Boredom's always a good sign." He gestured to the flat screen television mounted directly on the wall across from the foot of the bed. "You can watch all your favorite shows." When I rolled my eyes, he waved toward the windows. This room had windows facing in two directions, one looking out into some trees behind the resort, and the other offering a partial view of the field with mountains and the ocean in the distance. "At least you have a good view."

I bit back my retort. Despite my frustration, I wasn't going to cast aspersions on the view here.

His lips twitched with a smile. "Hang in there. You're on the mend. How's your pain?" he asked.

I wanted to growl, but that didn't seem reasonable. Like Flynn, Diego knew of my brief brush with opiate addiction.

"It's fine."

Diego gave me a long look, and I forced myself not to look away even though I wanted to. He was a good friend, the best kind of friend, the kind who always had your back. He was also perceptive as all hell, which sometimes drove me insane.

"Good. You don't have to be an ass to everybody."

"I'm not," I protested.

One of Diego's brows hitched up. "Man, your baseline is bordering on being an ass. If you need anything, let me know."

At that moment, the door to my bedroom opened —again—and Nora, Flynn's sister entered. "Hey," she said, her eyes bouncing from me to Diego. "Why do you have a pillow on your lap?"

Diego shrugged, casting her a quick grin. "We had a pillow fight, and Elias lost."

Nora laughed softly. Crossing the room, she held up a mug. "Fresh coffee. It won't be as good as Cammi's Red Truck coffee, but Daphne made it extra strong just for you."

I held up my hand, curling my fingers around the mug handle as she released it. I took a big swallow, closing my eyes as the rich flavor slid across my tongue. "That's delicious, thank you," I said as I opened my eyes.

Nora's brown hair was pulled up in a ponytail, and it bounced when she slid her hips on the foot of my bed. Her eyes matched her hair, and she was the only one of the Walker siblings who had those brown eyes. They coasted over me. "How's your pain?"

"Oh, my fucking God," I muttered. "You're the third person who's asked me that in the last ten minutes. It's fine. Ibuprofen is amazing."

Nora's forehead creased as she looked at me. "No need to be so irritable. You had a piece of plane metal puncture you in the side. It's kind of serious. I just want to make sure you're comfortable."

I felt a twinge of guilt at my irritation. "I'm comfortable. I promise. I will lay in this bed like a good boy and watch TV and hopefully be off these crutches soon."

"Have you had a shower yet today?"

My alarm must've shown on my face because she laughed. "I'm not planning to give you a shower. I just didn't know if you needed help getting in and out."

Diego threw his head back with a laugh. "Like he'd let any of us help him."

Nora gave me a concerned look. "Don't be stupid. We have the instructions for the bag thing you're supposed to put over your cast."

"I know, I know," I said with a sigh. All of my friends were trying to help, and I hated needing help. "Let me enjoy my coffee and have one of the fresh muffins Daphne's making, and then I wouldn't mind a little help."

Chapter Four

CAMMI

The little toddler in my lap yanked at my hair, letting out a squeal when her fingers curled tightly around a clump of it.

"Easy now," I said as I lightly gripped her hand, distracting her with a giant stuffed giraffe.

My friend's daughter, Iris, grabbed the giraffe before clambering off my knees where I was seated on the floor. Susie Winters looked over with a grin. "That's why my hair is always up," she said, gesturing to her brown curls pulled up high in a ponytail.

"Hazards of having a toddler, I suppose," I replied as I uncurled my legs and stood from the floor. I crossed the room to sit at the table where Susie was tapping away on her laptop.

Susie was a good friend. We'd grown up together in Diamond Creek. Lately, it seemed as if her life was moving at hyper speed, while my life felt stuck as I spun my wheels and went nowhere.

"What are you working on?" I asked as I smoothed my hand over my hair.

Susie reflexively looked over toward her daughter.

Iris was sitting on the floor, the giraffe now discarded at her hips as she played with some wooden blocks. Glancing back toward me, Susie replied, "Accounting. That's all I ever do. Today, I'm actually doing the books for Jared and his brothers. Quarterly reports are coming next month, and I like to have everything lined up early. I have to nag most of my clients."

"I bet you don't have to nag Jared," I teased lightly.

As if conjured by our discussion, Susie's husband came through the front door. "Hey ladies," he called. Jared Winters pushed the sunglasses up on his head, striding quickly across the room to give Susie a kiss. It was brief, but his lips lingered, and I felt myself looking away as if I were accidentally interrupting an intimate moment.

Jared was on the move, aiming for Iris and asking, "How's it going, Cammi?" He lifted their daughter into his arms. She squealed, patting his cheek with her small hand. "Hey, you." He gave her an exaggerated kiss on her cheek, and she curled her hand around the collar of his black T-shirt.

"Doing okay," I replied as he returned to stand beside the table. "Good grief, she looks so much like you."

Jared had rich green eyes and dark hair. He was classically handsome and could give off an intimidating vibe, mostly because he could come off on the stern and broody side. Iris shared his green eyes and glossy dark hair.

"I know, right?" Susie said with a grin. "No worries about who's the father."

Jared slid his eyes sideways. "As if there ever was."

Susie rolled her own eyes. "Don't get cocky."

I laughed, trying to ignore the twinge of jealousy I felt. I wasn't jealous specifically of Jared, and I adored

Susie, but I wanted my own family, and that wasn't looking like a possibility anytime in the near future. I had epically bad luck with men and was still recovering from my last disaster.

"Jay down for a nap?" Jared asked.

Susie nodded. "Yup. He crashed not long after Cammi got here." She lifted the baby monitor from where it sat on the table by her elbow. "We'll hear when he wakes up." Iris was their oldest child at two, and they also had a one-year old boy named after Jared who they called Jay.

When his daughter wiggled to be let down, Jared eased her to the floor and she toddled off to play with her blocks again. "How are the books looking?" he asked.

"Perfect. Because I do them," Susie replied with a sly grin.

Jared chuckled. "Another reason in the long list of reasons why I love you. I'm only here for a few minutes. I forgot the battery died in one of our boats, so I need to grab one out of the garage. Pizza for dinner? I can pick it up on the way home."

"Sounds good to me."

Jared gave Susie another kiss, waved to me, and then he hurried off into the garage to fetch the battery.

I looked over at Susie. "It's hard to believe you could hardly stand that man at one point."

Her smile was wide." I know, right? He still drives me a little nuts. He's such a perfectionist."

"The way you are with numbers, you should under-stand," I chided her gently.

Her brown eyes twinkled as she looked over at me. "True. Plus, having kids has chilled him out. You can only keep the house so clean."

I looked around, feeling another pinch in my heart, an almost stinging sensation over my breastbone. I ran my knuckles over it, quickly dropping my hand as soon as I realized what I was doing. I was jealous of a messy living room with toys scattered on the floor. I wanted this kind of disorder in my life, the loving mess of a family.

"Are you okay?" Susie asked, her voice bright.

Of course she noticed I was feeling melancholy. She knew me too well. Good friends were wonderful, but sometimes you wanted to hide from how much they saw through you.

"I'm fine," I replied with a light shrug. I took a sip of the water I'd left on the table earlier, hoping Susie didn't press.

I should've known better. She always pressed. She had the kind of personality that charged ahead, no matter what it was. "You're not fine." She closed her laptop, giving me her full attention. "What's up?"

My nose itched, and I rubbed my knuckles over it, masking my nervousness and discomfort. "I don't know. I feel like life is leaving me behind," I finally said.

Susie looked at me quietly for a moment before asking, "You're not still worried about what happened, are you? There's no way you could've known."

I bit my bottom lip, dread coating the insides of my stomach. My last attempt at a relationship had exploded in my face. When the man I thought was fine turned out to have an entire family in another town, and his wife showed up at my coffee truck with the kids in tow to rub it in my face that I was nothing more than a stupid cheater, well, it messed with my head in a big way. That had been months and months ago, but it still stung.

"I should've known," I protested.

"How? If you had somebody do a background check on him, it wouldn't have mattered. He gave you a fake name, so even doing a random online search wouldn't have helped. Sweetie, you can't go through life blaming yourself for not knowing he was lying. That's just crazy. It's a miserable way to live."

"Maybe. I thought I was falling in love with someone, but it turned out he had another whole family. I feel so stupid and awful."

"He hasn't called you again, has he?" she asked, her tone low.

Susie was a fiercely protective friend and would probably beat this guy up if given the chance. I loved that about her, but sometimes, it was a bit much.

"No. I've blocked him from every channel possible and changed my number. I just feel awful. I'm not that kind of person. I'm not an affair person."

"And everybody who matters knows that. He lied to you too. I hope for his wife's sake that she figures the whole story out at some point." She paused, tilting her head to the side as she regarded me. "You know what?"

"What?"

"We need to have a girls' night out. It's been months. Life has been so busy, we haven't made the time. How about tomorrow?"

"What if I have plans?" I countered, simply to be difficult.

Susie glared at me as she reached for her phone on the table.

"I'm sending a group text. You do *not* have plans. Well, now you do. With us."

"Where are we going?"

"You pick. The lodge restaurant, or Sally's."

I pretended to think about it for a minute. "The lodge. I want the yummy cider."

Her grin was wide. "Perfect. I'll drive, so you can get sloshed."

"If it doesn't work for tomorrow, let's make sure to make it happen soon," I said as I stood from the table. The group text she'd just sent to some of our friends flashed on my phone screen. I *did* want to spend time with friends, but I still felt glum and wanted to shake the feeling loose.

Susie followed me to the door, her eyes worried. "I feel like you're not bouncing back from this, Cammi. I don't know what to do. You're like a car I can't jump-start."

"I'm a car?" I returned, exasperated at the comparison.

"Obviously you're not a car, but you get my point."

I looked at my friend's familiar face—her wide brown eyes and her freckled cheeks. Her bubbly personality was blended with a strength and occasionally overwhelming staunch support that made her an incredible friend. "I'll make it through this. I'm not hung up on him. I just need to stop wishing for something I don't have," I assured her.

"It's been over six months," she said softly. "You haven't gone on a single date. Tess even tried to set you up with that guy she met in Anchorage."

I rolled my eyes. "He was totally not my type. I can't do the salesman thing."

"Don't judge," Susie protested. "Tess met him because he's a great fundraiser. He was helping her with that fundraiser for the hospital, and they made a ton of money.

"Okay, okay," I muttered. "It's not the salesman thing. It's just there was absolutely no oomph."

"Oomph?"

"You know what I mean. Even when you hated Jared, the room practically caught on fire when the two of you were together. There was zero chemistry for me with that guy. I'm not going to waste my time if I can't even imagine kissing a guy. I need to feel something."

She sighed. "Fair enough. We'll plan when we all get together."

"I'm not a group project," I warned. I glanced at my watch. "Look, I have to go. I need to pick up some supplies for the coffee truck tomorrow morning. Amy's covering this afternoon, but I also need to get there and help her close up."

"Aren't you about due to close for the season soon?" she asked, referring to the fact I closed my coffee truck for a few months every winter.

I nodded. "Soon, but you know I never have a set date. Business is slowing, but it's still steady."

Susie pulled me in for one of her fierce hugs and waved me off.

Chapter Five

ELIAS

Four months later - March

"Oh, for fuck's sake, I muttered, as one of my crutches dropped to the ground when I lost my grip.

Diego materialized at my side. "Got it." He lifted it from the ground and handed it to me.

"Thanks, man."

I hitched the crutch back under my arm. After adjusting my balance, I crutched along beside him as we got in line at Red Truck Coffee. The moment I looked up and saw Cammi moving swiftly as she took cash in one hand and turned to pull another shot of espresso with the other, my heart gave a swift kick. Something about her coming to visit me in the hospital had knocked me off balance a little. I didn't like to admit it, definitely not, but she'd feathered along in the edges of my thoughts ever since.

She'd been so sweet to bring me coffee. Not once, but twice. But then, Cammi was sweet.

Right. Exactly why she'll never give you a real chance. Not if she knows you were hooked on pills once.

I kicked that train of thought to the curb fast. It didn't matter that my addiction had been short-lived. I couldn't shake the nagging guilt. Plus, the list of reasons why someone who reminded me of sunshine and flowers wasn't suited for me was a hell of a lot longer than that.

"Bet you're itching to fly again," Diego commented from my side.

"Course I am. I fucking hate being grounded. I thought I was in the clear, but then they had to fix the pin," I replied. My healing had been dragged beyond the initial eight weeks after the pin didn't stay in place in my repaired ankle. Now, I was looking ahead and hoping I'd finally get my freedom back.

I crutched my way forward when the line moved, thinking I had a doctor's appointment soon and wondering when I'd get my cast off. A gust of salty air blew across the parking area, sending a stack of napkins in a swirl through the air. I started to move reflexively and came up short right before I landed the heel of my supportive cast on the ground.

Diego was already ahead of me. In two quick strides, he caught most of the napkins, with only one or two blowing loose. A seagull swept by, actually catching one of the loose napkins in its beak before shaking it free as soon as it discovered the napkin definitely wasn't food.

Diego held the napkins in his hand when he returned by my side. "Cammi's opened early this year," he commented.

"It's March," I replied.

"Yeah, but it's still cold. Climate change may be

coming, but we still have some cold days in March in Alaska." He chuckled when he cast me a quick look.

It *was* chilly, and I found myself wondering if Cammi was cold. Her red baker's truck had the name Red Truck Coffee painted on it in a whimsical script. You couldn't miss her truck when you were turning down the road to Otter Cove Harbor.

When we got to the front of the line, Cammi's blue eyes twinkled as she cast a quick smile between us. "Hey, boys. Good to see you." Her eyes lingered on me. "How are you doing, Elias? You better be following doctor's orders. I'm counting on a personal scenic flight from you when you can fly again."

"I promise I'm following doctor's orders," I said, lifting my hand and crossing it over my heart.

Cammi's smile felt like a ray of sun beaming inside my heart.

Diego chimed in. "He is, but he's working on getting a medal for being a grump about it."

"I imagine it's not fun being laid up," Cammi replied.

"I've got Daphne feeding me, which makes it easier. If I don't gain fifty pounds before this is over, it'll be a miracle."

Diego laughed. "True story. Your coffee is better than Daphne's though," Diego said, as if he needed to reassure her.

Cammi laughed. "I know Daphne's an amazing cook. If her coffee is as good as mine, I won't take it personally. Will it be the usual for both of you?"

"Yup," Diego replied quickly, his eyes flicking to mine.

I nodded. "Of course."

Cammi had our coffees ready in a jiffy. Diego didn't

even give me a chance to pay. I nudged him with my elbow, commenting, "My treat next time."

I took a swallow and closed my eyes. "Amazing," I said as I opened them to find Cammi's pretty eyes waiting.

Her smile unfurled slowly, and my heart gave another kick to my ribs. There was a line behind us, so much as I wanted to linger, we couldn't. "Come back soon," she called as we turned away.

"Always," Diego replied in return as he took my coffee from me.

"I can carry it," I protested.

Diego stopped, his brows hitching up. "Do you want to spill it? Because I couldn't carry it if I was trying to walk with crutches. Not worth trying to be a man about that."

I grumbled something in return before nodding. Because it *wasn't* worth spilling my coffee. "One more week," I said as I eased my legs into Diego's truck.

After we got my crutches put away, he handed me my coffee and started the engine. "Are you sure about that?"

"That's what the doctor said. I'm going to hold him to it."

Diego began driving, heading out to the harbor. He was picking up something for Flynn from Nathan Winters. Nathan Winters and his two brothers ran a fishing charter business. They often routed customers our way, and we did the same in return for them.

I looked out the window, taking in the view. It was only March, and the mountains across the bay were still covered in snow, the peaks jagged and tipped with white against the bright blue sky. The wind was up, ruffling the surface of the water. An eagle was flying nearby, coasting on the gusts of wind. I didn't think I'd ever get used to seeing eagles as much as I did here. They were massive, majestic birds and mighty fierce. Every time I got a close look at their fierce eyes, all I could think was I would *not* want to be a field mouse, or a salmon in the water when an eagle came at me with that look.

"So, when you finally gonna crack and ask Cammi out?" Diego asked conversationally.

My head whipped in his direction. "What are you talking about?"

He turned the steering wheel with one hand into the harbor parking lot as he replied, "Dude, you've had a crush on her forever. I think she likes you too. Might cheer you up."

"Shut the fuck up," I muttered.

Diego simply chuckled. He put his truck in park. "I'm gonna leave it running, so you don't freeze. Be right back."

He jogged off, and I shifted my shoulders. I took another swallow of coffee, and immediately thought of Cammi. I liked to think I wasn't too easy to read. For the most part, I wasn't. Except for my friends. Diego was right about me having the hots for her, but he didn't have enough sense to know I wasn't cut out for a girl like her.

———

A few hours later

"Be right back," Diego said as he climbed out of his truck—again.

I was discovering hitching a ride while Diego did errands wasn't turning out to be my best choice. It was nice to get out of the house, but I wanted to be able to move around more.

Of course, staying back home had me feeling more helpless. I wasn't going to feel better about my situation until I had my cast off and could at least get out and about on my own. I was beyond relieved that I was dealing with a broken left ankle. At least I'd be able to drive as soon as I had the cast off.

I drained the coffee, tracing my thumb over the label—Red Truck Coffee. Why did I have to go and have a crush on the girl who made the best coffee in town? It was inconvenient.

As if I conjured her by thought alone, when I glanced out the passenger side window, I saw Cammi coming out of the grocery store. Her arms were overloaded with bags. She was aiming in my direction, and I presumed she was parked nearby. Although her coffee truck was distinct, I didn't actually know what she drove personally.

In another moment, she was stopping at the small SUV parked beside us. She hadn't even seen me yet. "Oh, shit!" she exclaimed when she dropped a bag of groceries. A cloud of white flour puffed in the air.

Without thinking, I climbed out of the truck, grabbing one of my crutches out of the back to keep my balance. "Let me help," I commented.

Cammi looked up at me from where she'd knelt down. Her hair was dusted in white. "Oh, hey, Elias."

I felt my lips kicking up at the corners. Cammi didn't seem all that upset about dropping flour and getting it all over her hair. Looking down at the ground, I saw the flour was a lost cause. The paper bag had split wide open with flour spilling all over the pavement. "Let me get some of your bags," I said.

Cammi started to protest, "Elias, I've got it. You're on crutches."

She must've seen the frustration on my face because she corrected quickly, "Okay, here you go." She handed over one armload of bags.

Holding those in my free arm, I opened the back door, depositing the bags on the seat there. When I turned back, she was brushing her hand over her hair. She looked up. "How bad do I look?"

"I think it's kind of impossible for you to look bad, Cammi," I answered honestly.

Her cheeks went pink, and I suddenly became aware we were standing right beside each other. Electricity sizzled through me, awareness and my need for her sparking to life instantly.

I tore my eyes from hers for a moment, and they landed on the flour on the ground beside our feet. As my eyes lifted again, I realized she was still holding some grocery bags in her other hand. Without thinking, I reached for them. My fingers brushed hers, and streaks of fire chased over my skin just from that subtle touch.

"I've got these," I murmured, my voice coming out gruff.

Her fingers uncurled from the handles, and I took the bags from her, putting them beside the rest in the back. When I looked back toward her, she said incongruously, "I have a dustpan in the back."

I wasn't sure what that had to do with anything, and I wanted to tell her I would get it, but I seemed frozen. I could see the flutter of her pulse along the side of her throat and heard the whisper-soft intake of her breath. My eyes fell to her mouth and lingered on the little dimple on her bottom lip. My need to kiss her was *fierce*.

Chapter Six

CAMMI

Elias stared down at me, his eyes like dark chocolate. He searched my gaze quietly. My cheeks were burning hot, and my pulse had gone crazy. I tried to take a breath, but air was in short supply. Which made absolutely no sense, seeing as we were standing outside on a windy, late winter afternoon. There was more than enough fresh, crisp air, but I couldn't seem to get more than a shallow breath.

I felt his eyes dip down to my lips and unconsciously slid my tongue across them. His gaze whipped back up to mine, almost incredulous. "Did you really just do that?"

"Do what?"

I was pretty sure Elias actually growled. He tore his eyes from mine, leaning his head back to stare into the sky as he took a deep breath. My eyes were drawn to the divot at the base of his throat. Even though it was toward the end of winter, somehow his skin was still bronzed.

My brain cells seemed to have taken themselves out of commission because what I did next was crazy.

I leaned up and pressed a kiss right there in that divot. His skin was warm, and I caught the scent of him, musky and woodsy with a hint of the ocean clinging to him.

I lifted my lips from his skin reluctantly. Then, I knew I was crazy because when I looked up, I found him staring down at me, his gaze pure fire. At his look alone, my insides went molten.

He muttered, "Fuck it," right before dipping his head and dusting his lips across mine—once, twice, and then he fit his mouth over mine.

With each touch, it felt as if bolts of lightning were striking in the air around us. I gasped and stepped closer, sliding my palm up over his chest, stopping over his heartbeat. Sweet hell. I had fantasized about Elias whenever I let my guard down, but not one single fantasy came close to the real thing. His kiss was sure and commanding. His lips molded to mine, coaxing gently before sweeping his tongue to glide sensually against mine.

I was made of need, and I leaned into him, letting out a moan into our kiss. I felt him adjust his weight on his feet, noticing a subtle flinch when my hand slid unconsciously down his side.

I abruptly drew back and immediately apologized. "I'm sorry, did I hurt you?"

"Absolutely not," he said slowly, his eyes intent on mine. "But we *are* in a parking lot."

I jumped back, almost stumbling over the broken bag of flour at my feet. Then, I remembered I had flour in my hair. That's what I got for trying to carry too many bags at once. I took a shaky breath, willing myself to get a grip. I wished, I freaking wished, I could play this cool. But I'd never been good at playing anything cool. Not even a little.

I started to move, but realized Elias was standing right in my path. We were between the truck he'd been sitting in and my SUV. There wasn't exactly tons of space.

"I should get a dustpan," I finally announced.

Darting around the front of my SUV, I circled around to open the back. Just then, I heard Diego's voice, "What the hell did you do to the flour?" he drawled.

"It's my fault," I called as I popped out from behind my SUV with my dustpan and sweeper in hand.

Diego flashed me a quick smile. "Need some help?"

"I was helping her put away the groceries," Elias interjected.

"Is that why there's flour on the ground?" Diego teased as he opened the cab to his truck and dropped in several bags of groceries.

"No," Elias returned, his expression getting all grumpy.

When Diego came to stand beside us, I added, "I carried too much at once and dropped a bag. Elias got out and helped me get the rest put away."

"Do you always keep a dustpan and a broom with you?" Diego asked, his gaze puzzled.

I put a hand on my hip. "You never know when you might need them."

Diego chuckled. "Uh, I suppose so."

"I'll get out of your way," Elias said, moving swiftly with support of the one crutch to get back into the passenger seat of Diego's truck.

I quickly swept up the flour, straightening to find Diego waiting at the front of his truck.

"You all set?" he asked with a subtle lift of his chin. Diego was ridiculously handsome with rumpled dark curls, flashing green eyes, and a body worth drooling over. I appreciated him in an objective sense, but he didn't have the tendency to set my nerves alight the way Elias did.

"Of course. Just gonna dump this in the trash and go get another bag of flour."

"I'm sure I'll see you soon for coffee," he replied with a wink.

He turned and climbed in the driver's seat. I leaned over to pick up my purse where it had fallen on the ground. As I straightened, my eyes landed on Elias. He rolled down his window. "Don't forget you have flour in your hair."

My cheeks burned and butterflies spun in my belly at the teasing heat in his eyes.

Chapter Seven

ELIAS

Two weeks later

"Elias!"

At the sound of that cheerful voice, I turned, catching sight of Violet Hamilton. I'd gotten to know Violet pretty well because she'd drawn my blood several times over the last few months.

"Hey, Vi," I said as I paused in the hallway at the hospital

"You're looking good," she said as she stopped in front of me with a bright smile. Her dark hair was pulled back, and she wore a neon pink scrubs top with a ponytail holder to match. "No cast." She glanced down at my left foot before lifting her hand for a high five.

I smacked my palm against hers as I chuckled. "Finally."

"I'm glad. I know it got frustrating with that setback," she replied.

"I hope I never break my ankle again," I said fervently.

"Right, ankle breaks are a pain in the a—" She paused, correcting herself with, "bum."

I must've looked confused because she laughed. "Hazards of having a toddler. I try not to swear too much."

"Is "ass" technically a swear?"

Violet shrugged. "I don't actually know, but I don't want Alec to say it, so I'm gonna stick with "bum"," she explained.

I nodded. "Fair enough. How's it going?"

"Busy. Work is busy, and things are picking up at the ski lodge, so Sawyer's schedule has exploded." She was married to Sawyer Hamilton who owned the local ski lodge with his siblings.

"With the snow melting, ski season should be winding down, right?"

"It hasn't melted yet. Plus, they do all that hiking and biking stuff now, so they're busy all the time. Sawyer says they send people your way all the time for flight trips."

"They sure do, and we appreciate it."

Violet's name was paged over the hospital intercom. "Gotta run," she said quickly. "Off to stab someone with a needle. You take care." She hurried off, waving over her shoulder.

I resumed walking down toward the physical therapist's office. He had recommended a massage for me to help loosen up the tension around my knee and hip from compensating due to the problems with my ankle. At this point, I just wanted to be back to full speed, although I was flying again, so I wasn't going to complain.

A moment later, the receptionist smiled up at me.

The physical therapy and massage therapy offices were housed in an old wing of the hospital.

"Hey there, Elias," Claudia said with a soft smile.

"Hey, Claudia. Dan scheduled me with the massage therapist. I don't have a name though."

Claudia clicked on her keyboard, her eyes scanning the computer screen in front of her. "There you are. You've got an appointment with Cammi."

I only knew one Cammi, but figured it couldn't be the same one. "I hope this massage therapist is as good as the coffee at Cammi's Red Truck Coffee," I quipped.

"It's the same Cammi," Claudia said.

"It is?"

Claudia nodded just as the phone rang. Since I didn't want to look like an idiot standing there with my mouth open, I stuffed my hands in my pockets and turned to sit in one of the chairs in the small waiting area. I presumed the space was intended to be soothing with soft blue walls and watercolors of flowers. Meanwhile, I was grappling with the knowledge that Cammi would be giving me a massage. The mere idea of it sent electricity zipping through my body. I hadn't seen Cammi since that foolish kiss in the parking lot a few weeks ago.

I didn't like admitting it, to anyone, much less myself, but I'd replayed that kiss in my mind hundreds of times since then.

"Elias?"

I glanced over to see Cammi standing in the doorway to the waiting area. I stood and quickly crossed the room to her. Pink crested on her cheeks as I got closer.

"Come on back." She gestured for me to follow her.

A moment later, we were standing inside a small room. A massage table took up the entire center of the room, and it was otherwise almost empty, save for a chair in the corner and a small cabinet against the wall to the side of the table.

Cammi's scent hit me, some kind of flower with a hint of sweetness to it. I instantly recalled the feel of her lips underneath mine.

She twisted her hands, her brows arching slightly with a twitch of worry appearing between them. "I didn't realize I had an appointment with you. The physical therapy office handles my schedule."

"I didn't know you even did this."

Cammi shrugged. "It's a side gig. Helps me cover the bills during the winter when my coffee truck is closed down. I only do it part time, and then stop altogether in the summer," she explained.

Part of me wanted to leave because I didn't know if I could handle having her hands on my body. The physical therapist had talked me into this, as it was. Yet, her anxiety about it somehow pushed me. I wasn't going to chicken out.

As she stood there, I asked, "Is there a problem?"

"No." She shook her head quickly. "Unless you think there's a problem"

"I don't think there's a problem," I lied.

I supposed it wasn't a total lie. The only problem was me and my body's reaction to Cammi. Surely, I could handle that.

"Okay then," she said brightly. "I just need you to strip down to your underwear. You can put everything on the chair there." She gestured vaguely in the direction of the corner where the chair sat innocuously, oblivious to the undercurrents zinging back and forth in the air. "I'll be right back. You can lay face down on the table." She patted it and hurried past me.

"Didn't think I'd ever hear you asking me to strip." Those words just slipped out of my mouth.

Cammi spun back, her mouth opening slightly and pink cresting high on her cheeks again. She pressed her lips together in a line. "I didn't mean it like that."

I didn't know what the hell had gotten into me. I just wanted to ruffle her even more. "I wouldn't mind if you did."

Cammi let out a flustered sigh, turning and leaving the room without even granting me a reply.

A few minutes later, I'd done as instructed. I heard a light knock on the door, followed by Cammi's voice, "Can I come in?"

"Of course," I called, my voice muffled through the face-rest of the massage table.

After I heard the door open and close, she asked, "Any music requests?"

"I get to choose?" I heard her moving around and resisted the urge to lift my head.

"Of course."

"You pick."

I heard her murmur something, and then some soothing seventies blues came on, of all things. Somehow, she'd picked my favorite era and type of music without knowing.

Another moment later, I heard her saying, "I'll start with your back."

Her palms rested at the base of my spine, sliding up in a smooth pass, the oil warm under her touch. Although it was pure heaven to have Cammi's hands on me for reasons that had nothing to do with this massage, I didn't realize how much stress was built up in my body. I had to bite back a groan at how good it felt to have her working the tension out of the corded muscles in my spine and shoulders before making her way to my glutes and then down my legs.

"Damn, I was more sore than I realized," I mumbled.

My entire upper left side was balled with tension. Cammi's touch was light but firm

"You've been compensating for your leg for months now. That takes a toll."

It wasn't until it was all over and I was practically jelly on the table that Cammi's voice came again. "I'll be back in a few minutes. I'll give you time to get dressed."

I lay there, almost undone. After a moment, I slowly rolled up, marveling at the absence of tension, especially in my spine and along that one leg. I definitely could've used a few more massages. I chuckled to myself as I got dressed with the Bee Gees playing in the background.

A few minutes later, there was another knock on the door. I was still sitting in the chair, although I was fully dressed now.

"It's safe," I called.

Cammi came in, her gaze sweeping over me. "How do you feel?"

"Better than I have in months."

Her lips twisted to the side with a half-smile. "Good. You could use a little relaxation, you know," she teased lightly.

"Well, Dan 'prescribed' it," I said, using air quotes as I stood from the chair.

"Make sure to drink plenty of water. You might experience some soreness after the fact. The water will help."

"Yes, ma'am," I replied, dipping my head in acknowledgment.

The room suddenly felt small, and the air lit with a humming charge. My rational side knew kissing Cammi again was a bad plan, but reason didn't hold much power in the moment.

Stepping closer, I searched her eyes, watching as they darkened like the sky on a stormy day, the blue deepening to almost navy. Her lips parted with a breath, and that soft sound was like a match tossed in dry leaves.

I didn't realize I was standing so close until she took a deeper breath and I felt the brush of her breasts against my chest. As if she could read my mind, she whispered, "This is a bad idea."

"Maybe," I murmured.

I waited, although I didn't know why. When her tongue darted out to swipe across her bottom lip, I was gone. Decision made.

Her hair was up in a bun with loose tendrils dangling around her cheeks. Lifting a hand, I brushed one back, the lock of hair sliding like silk through my fingers. I dropped a kiss on one corner of her mouth, and then the other, capturing her gasp with my lips when I fit my mouth over hers.

She made this little throaty sound. It was like spurs in the flanks of my desire. Closing the inch between us, I slid one palm down her spine into the dip of her waist and over the sweet curve of her bottom, pulling her into a full body clench as I deepened our kiss.

Kissing Cammi was dangerous. I dove into the sweet heat of our kiss, her tongue gliding like liquid silk. She made a little impatient sound, flexing into me as one hand curved over my shoulder to cup the back of my neck and pull me closer. Her tongue was bossy against mine and for a few moments there, I lost sense of everything but her.

She was intoxicating. I finally needed air, and broke my lips free, leaning my head back and gulping it in, inhaling her scent, which only served to cloud the haze of lust in my mind. I could feel the press of her nipples against my chest with every ragged breath she took.

Looking back at her, all my cells were scrambled, and I couldn't think. Cammi, sweet Cammi, was something else when she let her guard down. Her cheeks were flushed pretty and pink, and her lips plumped and swollen from our kiss.

I shocked myself with what I said next. "I want to see you."

"I'm right here," she murmured.

"No, I mean not just a kiss."

She swallowed, and something flickered in her eyes. Worry, I thought.

We stared at each other in the quiet, and then Cammi jumped when there was a knock on the door. "Your next appointment is here," Claudia's voice called through the door.

"Be right there," she called in return.

Cammi was all in a fluttery hurry then. "Okay, um. Claudia will schedule you. I'm not sure if the next one will be with me, or somebody else."

She practically shoved me out the door, while I tried to absorb the implications of the fact that it seemed I couldn't get too close to Cammi without kissing her.

Chapter Eight

CAMMI

"Finally," Susie said as she looked around the booth.

Tess grinned at her. "Finally, what?"

"We're finally having girls' night. Every time we've tried, we either reschedule or only some of us make it. I sent that first group text about four months ago. Everybody's too busy," Susie grumbled as she shrugged out of her jacket.

We were at Last Frontier Lodge, Diamond Creek's high-end ski and adventure lodge, which also happened to have a fabulous restaurant.

"Three of the nights that were suggested, you had a conflict," Hannah said, rolling her eyes from across the table.

"It's hard. Finding a babysitter feels like an act of God sometimes," Susie replied.

I looked around at my friends. Along with Susie, Tess, and Hannah, Emma had also joined us. Susie, Hannah, and I had all grown up in Diamond Creek together. Emma moved here about five years ago. She was Hannah's biological sister who'd been adopted before Hannah was even born. Tess had shown up here on vacation and fallen in love with Nathan Winters. Nathan, along with his brothers, Jared and Luke, owned a fishing charter business. With Susie married to Jared and Hannah married to Luke, Tess was in the thick of that family mix.

Emma was married to Trey Holden. He was an attorney and also a pilot who happened to be friends with Elias. Elias, who I seemed to have developed a habit of kissing, if two times counted as a habit.

Hannah flicked Susie a quick look. "I don't know what I'd do without your mom."

"She's a godsend when it comes to babysitting, even if she's not available all the time," Susie said. She lifted her hand and pulled out the elastic holding her curls up, and they fell in a rumple around her shoulders.

Emma grinned. "Trey's my babysitter," she said.

"Trey is a saint," Tess added. "Plus, he's got a much better schedule than our husbands."

Emma smiled. "He does, and I'll never complain about it."

"With you about to have another baby, you'll be twice as grateful," Susie commented with a grin.

Emma replied, "No argument there." She absently rubbed her palm over her round belly. She was within a month of her due date and very pregnant.

It was moments like this that I was painfully reminded just how behind the ball I felt in my life. I wanted a baby, so, *so* much. I was already staring down thirty-three years old, and I had no potential father in sight. It felt like my biological clock had neon emergency alarms blaring. I knew it was all in my head, well not one-hundred percent. Hormones were definitely part of it. I could reason my way out of it, but it didn't change that I desperately wanted to complain about not having a babysitter, or how hard it was to find one, and have a partner whose work schedule was a nightmare. I'd happily take all of those pesky frustrations if it meant I had a family with someone.

Instead, I envied my friends, and I hated my envy because it made me feel childish. Needing a distraction as they commiserated over babysitting, I snatched a menu from where it was tucked between the condiments and opened it.

No one even noticed I wasn't part of the conversation, and I knew just how ridiculous I was being that even that hurt my feelings a little.

Blessedly, Delia Hamilton stopped by the table. "Hey, ladies." She had a water pitcher in hand and immediately began filling our glasses.

"Are you the hostess tonight?" I asked as I glanced up at her.

Delia was the chef and managed the restaurant here. She'd been a few years behind us in high school, but we all knew her. Her blue eyes twinkled with her smile, and her blond ponytail swung over her shoulder as she leaned over to fill our water glasses. "Just in a pinch," she replied. "Harry's out of town this week, so I'm taking over when things get a little hectic upfront. Kayla will be serving you, and she'll be out in a minute. Do you want to hear the specials though?"

"Absolutely," Tess said as she glanced up.

Delia quickly recited the specials.

"I already know what I want," Susie commented.

Delia grinned. "Kayla will be right here. I don't even have a notebook. I can promise you that I won't remember."

After Delia hurried off, Emma, always perceptive, caught my eyes. Susie and Hannah were looking at something on Susie's phone while Tess was texting someone.

"So, how have you been?" Emma asked. She and Hannah were strikingly similar in appearance. They were both tall and leggy with almost black hair that hung in straight glossy locks. Her blue eyes crinkled at the corners as she smiled over at me. I loved having Emma as a friend, but she was a therapist and sometimes too perceptive.

"I've been fine," I said with a light shrug. "The coffee truck is getting busy, and I need to cut back on my hours doing massages for the physical therapy office."

"Do you like doing that in the winter?"

"I do." The moment I said that, I recalled my appointment a few days ago with Elias. Dear God, that man made me feel all kinds of inappropriate.

"I need to get my doctor to recommend a massage," Susie interjected.

"You don't have to have a doctor's recommendation. You can schedule on your own."

"Yeah, but if my doctor refers me, then my insurance pays for it," Susie countered matter-of-factly.

"True," I replied with a grin.

Just then, a motion across the restaurant caught my eye. Looking over, I saw Elias walking in with Diego and Flynn. The moment my eyes landed on him, my belly did a spinning flip. Heat flooded my cheeks, and he hadn't even looked at me.

As if he could read my mind, his head turned and his eyes locked with mine instantly. I could feel the intensity of his gaze from all the way across the crowded restaurant. It felt as if a flame licked through the air between us, traveling on a fuse of desire.

"Well," Susie said. "Now that is a *look*."

I abruptly tore my eyes away from Elias, grabbing my water, taking a gulp and almost choking on a piece of ice in the process. Tess had to whack me on the back. "You okay?"

After I caught my breath, I nodded and took a slower sip of water. "Yeah, I'm fine."

"You were distracted by all that hotness," Susie chimed in.

"What are you talking about?" I asked, casting a glare at Susie.

"You having a stare down with Elias Lowe. He's totally hot. Like need-a-fan hot," she clarified.

I felt a fresh blush creep up my neck and into my face. I simply rolled my eyes. "Maybe so."

Susie flicked her eyes quickly across the room and blessedly, Elias, Flynn, and Diego were sitting down at a table and not looking our way. Glancing back toward me, Susie added, "That's it. You and Elias would be perfect together."

I narrowed my eyes. "Don't you dare start matchmaking for me."

Tess gave me a sympathetic look. "Susie loves to play matchmaker, and there's no one left."

Hannah caught my eye. "Ignore Susie."

"That's my plan. Now, can we talk about something other than my lack of love life?" By some miracle, I managed to keep my tone light.

Although Susie wrinkled her nose and cast me a slightly disgruntled look, she dropped it. It was good to spend time with my friends. We usually tried to get together as a group once a month, but since they'd all started having kids, it had been harder for our schedules to coordinate. It was hit or miss, and often it wasn't all of us. It just went to show how insanely busy we all were, myself included, even if I didn't have a husband and kids yet.

Dinner was delicious, and I was glad we managed to find time together. There was always plenty of gossip other than love lives to catch up on. The latest town scoop was that Misty Mountain Café was up for sale.

"You should buy it," Emma said firmly, her eyes on me.

"Me?" I squeaked.

"Yes. It's perfect. Your coffee is better than theirs. Don't get me wrong, when I need a place to sit down, I love going there, and they have great pastries. But owning that café would give you a year-round option. You make it work, but every winter you worry a little about money and kind of piece things together. This fits in well with your coffee truck, and you already have a great reputation in town," she explained.

Anticipation and anxiety spun through me. The idea grabbed onto me, but it was a major thing to consider. "I don't know. I like the idea, but my little coffee truck is a much smaller operation. This would be a big step, and I don't want to give up my coffee truck."

Tess brushed her honey gold curls away from her shoulders and gave me a steady look. "You can do this. I will help you come up with a business plan for the bank."

"And, I'll help you with the accounting." Susie already did the accounting for Red Truck Coffee, but that was small beans compared to Misty Mountain Café.

Glancing between my friends, the swirl of anticipation inside spun faster. "Okay, I'll think about it. I didn't even know they were selling. Do you know why?" I asked the table at large.

Hannah replied, "Yeah, Carol's mother is sick. Her family isn't from here, so they're going to move to be closer to her."

"Oh, wow. That's too bad." I leaned back in the booth.

"Change always happens. That's about the only thing that's guaranteed in life, trite though it may be," Emma offered.

After we finished dinner, and I hugged all of my friends goodbye, I took a restroom break before I headed out into the parking lot. My attention had occasionally been distracted by Elias across the restaurant, but the space was crowded enough that I didn't have a good line of sight during dinner. My eyes landed on him once more as I left, and I lifted my hand in a wave that I hoped looked casual. He returned the wave, his eyes lingering just long enough that my skin prickled.

As I walked toward the front, I noticed it was still partly light out with the sun leaving a splashy show of pinks and reds in the sky as it set. The days were getting longer. Since I'd grown up in Alaska, I didn't know what spring felt like in other places, but here, there was a sense of quickening. Time sped up as the days rapidly lengthened, and the tourists began to pour into town. The snow hadn't even melted yet everywhere, but everything felt as if it was moving faster.

There was a line in the waiting area at the restaurant, and I moved through quickly. Out of the corner of my eye, I sensed a motion and looked reflexively in that direction. My stomach plummeted to my feet the moment my eyes landed on my ex with his wife, the one I didn't know about. Hell, I hadn't even known his real name until after the whole mess blew up in my face.

Shock slammed into me and my feet got stuck in place. Unfortunately for me, another family was pushing past me on their way in and knocked me slightly off balance because I wasn't paying attention. My ex—who I had known as Brad—looked away to say something to his wife. His real name was Joel. His wife, Fran, stared at me, and her eyes felt like poison darts pinned on me. I felt absolutely awful, shame making my stomach roil.

I started moving again, but not fast enough. She closed the distance between us when there was a gap in the cluster of people waiting and stopped beside me, her eyes narrow and angry.

Joel, who I had a hard time not thinking of as Brad, crossed over, curling his hand around her arm. "Fran, leave it alone."

As if the universe had set out to make this situation as mortifying as possible, Elias, Diego, and Flynn appeared and paused at my side. The tension was obvious, at least to me. I didn't even know what Joel was doing here because he didn't live here.

"Everything okay?" Diego asked in an easy, friendly tone.

When I looked up at him, I couldn't even speak. As Joel dragged Fran away, she replied to Diego, "No, everything is *not* okay."

I wanted to melt into nothing. I swallowed through the tight knot of tears and shame in my throat and squeezing the life out of my lungs. "It's fine," I said, practically running out of the entrance area.

The cool evening air coasted over me as I stepped

outside, easing the hot shame pressing against my skin. When I reached my SUV, I started to get in, but then noticed it seemed to be listing slightly to one side. Glancing back, I saw one of my tires was flat.

"Fuck," I muttered to myself. I needed a minute, so I climbed in my SUV and leaned my forehead against the steering wheel. "Dammit." I bounced my forehead lightly on the padded edge of the steering wheel, feeling one tear, another, and then another roll in rapid succession down my cheeks.

I was over Joel, but I wasn't over my stupidity. I had an affair, and I didn't even know it was an affair. How stupid was that? Really, *really* stupid. I was devastated and so ashamed. To make this specific moment more aggravating, I had a flat tire.

There was a light knock on my window. I slowly opened my eyes, fearing it was Joel, or potentially worse, Fran. Actually, Fran would've been a better option. Because I could apologize again.

When I finally opened them, I found Elias peering at me through the window. I dragged my palms across my cheeks and reached for a tissue in the glove box, wishing he would maybe go away.

"Are you okay?" he called through the window, his voice slightly muffled.

No, I was definitely *not* okay, not even a little. But I didn't think Elias was going to leave. After a few breaths, I opened the door. "One of my tires is flat."

Elias's eyes searched my face quietly, and I wanted to squirm. I didn't need my crush witnessing me feeling so low.

"I noticed. That's why I came over to check," he finally said. "I'm parked right there." He gestured toward his truck, a navy-blue light duty truck. It suited him perfectly—practical and understated. "Do you have a spare tire?"

That was the logical question. It took me a minute to drag myself out of the mental rut I'd tumbled into after that shitty encounter on the way out.

"Yeah," I said, my voice coming out kind of raspy.

He stepped away as I moved to get out. I went around and opened the back, turning the little plastic latch and lifting up the section inside where my spare tire was stored. Except there was nothing there. I leaned my head back, staring into the sky. The beauty should've caught my notice. The sun was setting, and early spring sunsets in Alaska were glorious, the sky splashed with color. My brain barely registered it.

"No," I said as I brought my gaze level with Elias's. "I suppose I don't have a tire."

We looked together into that empty spot, shaped perfectly for a tire, except there was no tire there. Elias's eyes slid to mine. "Did you get this used? Or did you use the spare and forget to replace it?"

"I got it used last year and never even thought to check for that," I said with a tired sigh.

His lips quirked with a sympathetic smile. "Let me take a look at your tire. I've got an air thing in the back of my truck."

"An air thing?"

He shrugged lightly, drawing my attention to his shoulders as he walked to the back of his truck parked directly in front of my vehicle. God. He had great shoulders—muscled and fit, his dark navy T-shirt stretched across them. Although the air was cool, he seemed indifferent to it. He was that kind of guy. He probably threw off enough heat that he almost didn't need a jacket in the winter. Okay, maybe that was a little ridiculous.

I followed him over as he opened the back of his truck cab. It was filled with tools. "I thought you were a pilot," I offered.

"I am," he said as he cast me a quick grin, promptly sending my belly into a dizzying spin of flips. "But, I do a bunch of stuff. Never hurts to have tools."

"Okaa-ay," I said slowly.

"Let me take a look at that tire first." He walked back and knelt down beside the tire, sliding his palm over it in a smooth motion. Gah! I even thought his hands were sexy. I wondered how it would feel to have him slide his palm over my skin the way he slid it over the tire. A tire! I thought him checking my tire was sexy. Geez, I had it all kinds of bad.

His hands were strong and a little battered, like he knew how to make good use of them, which I was confident he did. He straightened, his brow wrinkling slightly when he looked at me. "Someone slashed that tire."

"What?" I squeaked.

He nodded solemnly. "Yeah." He leaned over, running his fingers over what I now saw to be a puncture in my tire. "Maybe I drove over something?"

I was so shocked I didn't realize how illogical that was. "It's on the side of your tire," he pointed out.

The dread and shame I'd felt when I'd seen Joel and Fran in the waiting area rolled through me again, and I felt sick. "Oh," was all I could manage.

"Let me take you home. I'll take care of your tire tomorrow."

"You don't—" I began, but I shut up real quick when Elias leveled me with a firm look.

"You don't have a spare tire, and I'm here. You can figure out your tire tomorrow."

I wanted to argue, but that was silly, and I knew it.

I let out the breath I hadn't realized I'd been holding and nodded. "Okay. Thank you."

I got my purse out of the SUV and locked it. I followed Elias to his truck where he insisted on getting the door for me. I felt unsettled and restless, wanting to run from all the feelings I had spinning inside. Instead, I buckled my seatbelt. He closed the door and rounded the front of his truck to climb in on the driver's side. I idly noticed he had a barely perceptible hitch in his gait. If I hadn't known he'd broken his ankle recently, I might not've noticed.

It was quiet for a few moments after he started his truck and drove down the winding drive from the ski lodge. When he reached the end of the driveway, he looked in my direction.

"What?" I prompted.

"I don't know where you live."

"Oh." I felt like an idiot. That seemed to be my theme tonight. "It's on the other side of town. You can go down the hill and through town toward the harbor."

"Yes, ma'am," he said with a nod.

He started driving, and tension spun so tight inside that my composure began to unravel. Tonight hadn't turned out so well. I took a breath and then another, grateful he wasn't trying to be chatty.

But then, chatty wasn't how I would've described Elias. He'd been coming to my coffee truck for years now, and I still didn't know a whole lot about him.

"How are you doing over there?" I asked, in an attempt to nudge me out of my own thoughts. When I glanced his way to find his eyes on me, just for a moment, the air felt as if it were suddenly lit by a hot charge.

"I'm doing okay. It's just a tire," he offered as he looked back toward the road.

"I know."

"What happened back there?"

I knew exactly what he was asking about, but I hedged anyway. "What do you mean?"

"On the way out. You seemed upset."

Fuck my life. I decided the only way out of this awkwardness was brutal honesty.

"I accidentally had an affair last year. I feel like shit. The guy and his wife were in the reception area. I didn't know it was an affair because he lied to me and even gave me a fake name. He lives up in Anchorage, but he has a summer business down here, so that's how we met. Last year was his first year in business, so I didn't know any better. I didn't know pretty much everything he told me was all bullshit. Long story short, I don't even know what he told her. As soon as I found out what I'd stumbled into, obviously, I completely ended things. I called her to apologize, but she seems to think I knew what I was doing. I still feel awful."

"Jesus, that sucks, Cammi. He's a fucking asshole."

"Yeah. I feel like the world's biggest idiot."

Elias was quiet for a moment, the sound of his blinker loud inside the truck as he came to a stop at the bottom of the hill. He looked my way, his eyes holding mine. The look there stole my breath and set my heart off at a rapid beat.

"You're not an idiot, and you didn't deserve that. Hell no. You can't be expected to go through life wondering if people are completely lying about who they are. That's no way to go about life. So, you trusted the wrong person. Happens to the best of us.

You're better than that, and you deserve so much more."

Okay, that was the most Elias had *ever* said to me in one shot. He exuded a sense of protectiveness and anger on my behalf. My heart flipped over. I blinked at the emotion rushing through me. "I know, but thanks for saying it."

He dipped his chin in acknowledgment and looked back toward the highway before turning onto it. That charge was still hovering in the air, and I could hear every beat of my heart echoing through my body. I felt hot, and my skin was prickly. I was hyper aware of Elias and I kept stealing glances at him. He drove with one hand resting on top of the steering wheel. My eyes traced the line down from his shoulder over his muscled forearm to his hand.

I tore my eyes away from his hand and they landed on his jaw. While Elias was definitely hot, like need-a-fan-hot as Susie described, he was beautiful. The lines of his profile were clean and strong, almost elegant. His nose was straight, and his cheekbones angled and cut. My eyes lingered hungrily on his lips. They were sensual and full, yet masculine.

Absolutely everything about Elias was masculine. He didn't even have to try to telegraph confidence, it oozed from him in an understated way.

"Cammi?"

His low voice almost made me jump. I'd zoned out that badly.

"Where should I turn? You said out past the road to the harbor, and the harbor is coming up," he added.

"Oh, sorry. Actually, do you mind stopping at my coffee truck?" I'd remembered to drop the cash bag off at the bank earlier, but I'd forgotten my laptop. I liked

to settle the numbers every night. "If it's a problem—"
I began.

Elias's eyes slid to mine, and he smiled slightly. "It's
not a problem."

He slowed and turned in at the harbor, immediately hooking a right into the small gravel parking lot
in front of my coffee truck.

"I meant to stop by on my way home. Obviously, I
wasn't planning on having someone slash my tire," I
murmured, feeling my cheeks go pink.

"Right. Most people don't expect that," he said
dryly.

The gravel crunched under his truck tires as he
came to a stop right in front of my little coffee truck.
I'd had this business for years now, and I still felt a
little surge of pride whenever I looked at my cute little
truck. I'd painted the whole thing myself, including
the sign, back when I got this truck at a sweet price. It
had been a small dream and seemed easy enough to
pull off when the city allowed me to rent the space at
such a low price. There had once been a gas station
here, but it burned down. The city cleaned up the lot,
and when I went to ask about parking my truck there,
they went for it. I loved my little business.

My mind started to skip over to my conversation
with my friends about buying the other main coffee
shop in town, but I pushed those thoughts away. I
needed to get my computer and get going since Elias
was my ride. I unbuckled my seatbelt and hopped out.
"Be right back."

I went to the back of the truck where the entrance
was, my footsteps slowing when I saw the door was
wide open.

I hadn't even realized Elias had followed me. "I just

noticed the door was open," he said when he stopped beside me. "Everything okay?"

I peered inside, flicking on the lights. My serving window, technically on the side of the truck, but the front of my business, was locked up tight. After my tire incident tonight, I was worried. I didn't like thinking it, but I feared my ex or his wife might've had something to do with my tire. Now this? But that was crazy-thinking. Brad, I mean Joel, wouldn't come here and break into my coffee truck. I couldn't imagine his wife doing that either.

I stepped inside with Elias right on my heels. I wasn't particularly worried about anyone being in here. There was absolutely nowhere to hide. Over the years, I'd had two break-ins, both times just kids being stupid and looking for cash. One night, the cops even found two teenage girls making coffee for their boyfriends. They were all high on marijuana and apparently giggled at being caught.

I scanned the space, not finding anything amiss. Then, there was a scuffling sound.

"What in the world?" I began slowly. Then, my eyes landed on the distinct rump of a porcupine trying to hide under the shelves. "Oh, God. The latch must've been loose."

"There's your burglar," Elias said with a chuckle.

The porcupine's bottom wiggled, and its quills were up. Despite their prickly reputation, which was deserved, porcupines were shy creatures.

"I'm guessing he was curious and maybe a little hungry. You do have those cookies and muffins."

"How do I get him out of here?" I mused.

We both stepped to the door, which was on the far end from where the porcupine was trying to appear invisible under a curtain that hung in front of the shelves. It was purple with tiny flowers on it. The sight of the prickly rump with the bright curtain draped over it was incongruous.

Elias cupped my elbow lightly. "Let's get out and push the door open wider. I'm guessing we can lure him out."

"We can?"

"Let's just see."

Elias and I climbed out and went around to the other end of the truck. He tapped lightly on the side of the truck near where the porcupine was inside. At that, we heard some motion. After some louder tapping, the porcupine clambered down the steps. Even when they were moving fast, porcupines didn't actually move very fast. This one waddled rapidly across the parking lot before disappearing into the trees on the far side.

I laughed. "Well, that was definitely better than getting quilled."

"Ever been quilled by a porcupine?" he asked as he followed me back into the truck.

"Actually, yes. I was a little girl, and a little too curious. It did hurt, but I only got two in me. You actually have to get right up close. The quills don't travel very far." I leaned over to fetch my laptop from its storage spot in a locked cabinet.

When I straightened, Elias commented, "Damn, just standing in here makes me want some coffee."

"I'll make you a coffee. Do you want one?"

"I'll never say no to your coffee," he said, so solemnly that I burst out laughing. "You don't have to though."

"Coming right up. It's the least I can do after you gave me a ride and saved me from a porcupine."

A gust of wind from the harbor nearby flew into the coffee truck, swinging the door shut with a thump.

"Do you want that open?" he asked.

"Nah. It's chilly out anyway. Now that I'm making coffee for you, we might as well be comfortable."

I tapped the button to turn on my industrial espresso machine and opened the cabinet above where I kept my supplies. "Your usual?"

"Of course."

I'd worked in my coffee truck with more than one person on many occasions. I often hired extra help in the summers. But this was the very first time I'd been in here late at night, alone with a man who I wanted to kiss so fiercely the desire was almost an ache in my body.

Elias leaned his hips against the narrow counter running along the wall behind where I made coffee. "It's very organized in here," he observed as his eyes scanned the space.

"I have to keep it organized. It's too small. Other-wise, it would be cluttered all the time."

I started his coffee and turned to rest my hips against the counter opposite him. There was only about two feet between us. His eyes traveled up and down, lingering on mine when they landed on my face again. My thoughts fuzzed, and the air felt in short supply. I almost forgot to turn off the coffee, but the machine blessedly beeped when his shot was done, and I turned to switch it off.

Only a minute later, I handed him a coffee. He moved to take his wallet out of his back pocket, and I waved him away. "Don't you dare. You're giving me a ride home."

Flustered with his presence, I busied myself cleaning up. I heard him take a swallow of coffee and then he let out a sound of pleasure. "Best. Coffee. Ever."

Turning, I smiled. "Really?"

Elias held my eyes and nodded. "Absolutely. That's why I come here every day I'm working on my way out to the plane hangar," he said flatly. He set the coffee on the counter and surprised me when he reached across the space between us and caught one of my hands in his.

Before I could even wonder what he was doing, he reeled me to him in a smooth motion. I was standing bracketed between his feet, and I could feel his muscled thighs on the outsides of my legs. He held my gaze just long enough that I almost looked away from the intensity. My pulse was galloping along, and I could hardly get any air into my lungs.

Then he went and lifted his hand, lightly cupping my chin and tracing his thumb across my bottom lip. My brain cells went up in smoke.

Chapter Nine

ELIAS

Cammi's eyes went dark. Her lips parted, and I wanted to kiss her so badly it hurt.

Although I hadn't let myself spend too much time with Cammi, the reason I'd always steered away from getting too close was because she had a sweetness about her, a kindness that ran bone deep. I kind of lost my mind when I heard the bullshit that guy pulled on her. I knew she would never set out to have an affair with someone. She was loyal through and through and exuded it in everything she did.

I felt deeply protective of her, and I wanted to beat the shit out of that fucking asshole who'd used her like that. I hated to think her natural kindness could be soiled by cynicism.

And, the plain truth was, I wanted her, so fiercely I was tired of trying to swim against the current of my raw desire.

"I'm going to kiss you now." My voice came out gruff, frayed by the need rushing through me.

Cammi's lashes brushed against her cheeks before

she lifted her eyes, slowly, searching mine. "Okay," she whispered.

Somewhere in this moment where I had lost all sense of time, I'd slipped an arm around her waist, my palm resting at the base of her spine. Because I was selfish and greedy and couldn't resist, I slid my hand down over the sweet curve of her bottom like I'd wanted to forever.

Cammi's breath hitched, and she made a little sound at the back of her throat as I nudged her closer. Her soft curves bumped against my body. Her scent, sugar and flowers, spun around me. I slid my hand around to cup the base of her neck. Her head tilted back just as I dipped to brush my lips across hers. I meant to start this kiss gently. That lasted all of a second, if that. The moment my lips touched hers, it felt as if a bolt of lightning struck my body.

Every cell lit on fire, and the only way to save myself from getting burned was to dive into it. I fit my mouth over hers, growling when she let out a sigh into our kiss. And then, I was devouring her with deep strokes of my tongue, which she met stroke for stroke as she flexed against me.

Any intentions I had—and I couldn't say I thought this through at *all*—flew out the window. I squeezed her bottom and then slid my hand up under her T-shirt, curling around her side to cup her breast. Her nipple pebbled under my touch through the thin silk of her bra, and I growled again as I brushed my thumb back and forth over it.

Fuck me. I needed more, and I needed it now. Cammi's hands were busy, one mapping my chest, and the other stealing under the hem of my shirt, her touch was warm against my skin. I tore free from her mouth, breathing in long gulps of air. When I looked down, her chest was heaving and her lips were damp with her skin flushed pink.

I brushed my thumb over her nipple again, and I felt her shift her thighs. I needed more.

With my eyes on hers, I dipped my head before letting my gaze break free to dust kisses along her collarbone, pressing a hot open kiss at the base of her throat. She gasped my name, and I dragged her shirt down, almost dying a little inside when I saw she was wearing a black lace bra. Her pink nipples teased me through the dark lace. I shoved it down, and her breast plumped up over the top. I laved my tongue over one nipple before sucking lightly, savoring her little gasp and the feel of her fingers spearing in my hair.

I wasn't going to take it that far tonight, but my cock was hard, to the point of pain. Sweet Cammi had tempted me for too long.

She had this penchant for wearing skirts. Thank fuck she had one on tonight, with boots of course. That was her style, kind of feminine and tomboy at once. I loved it. Moving swiftly, I pushed away from the counter and lifted her, sliding her hips onto the counter behind her, the very one where she'd served me coffee so many times.

I slid my palms up her legs, the fabric of her skirt rising up with my touch until it was in a rumple around her hips. "What are you doing" she whispered on the heels of a soft whimper when I cupped my palm between her thighs, feeling the damp silk there.

"You tell me. I can stop right now, or I can make you come all over my fingers and mouth."

Her eyes widened and her mouth dropped open. I took that as an opportunity to kiss her again. Her tongue was sassy with mine.

Drawing back, I prompted, "Tell me what you want."

"Well, I mean, when you put it like that." Her cheeks flushed a deeper shade of pink and her eyes fell.

"Look at me."

Those pretty blues met mine again. "What?" she whispered, lifting her chin slightly.

"Do you know how long I've wanted to do this?"

She shook her head.

"Since the first day I saw you." I let that fall between us, watching her eyes widen slightly and her breath come out in a startled puff. "Now, where was I?" I dipped my head and pressed kisses on her neck again. She liked that, arching and letting out a little whimper when I nipped lightly. Straightening, I added, "Just tell me to stop if you don't want this."

"Oh, there's no chance of that," she said, her voice husky. "I didn't let myself think too far, but I've wanted you ever since I saw you."

She bit her lip. I kissed her once, hard and fast, before letting my hand slide up the inside of her thigh again to tease over the damp silk. I pushed it aside, letting out a growl of satisfaction when I found her satiny, wet heat.

Cammi let out a ragged gasp as I teased my fingers through her slick folds. Lifting my eyes, I took her in. With her cheeks flushed pink, her breasts rising and falling with every breath she took, and her eyes darkening to navy, she was fucking glorious.

I dipped my head, nipping lightly at her earlobe. She arched her head, gasping when I sank two fingers in her channel. I needed to taste her sweet mouth, so I made my way there, dropping hot kisses along her neck before capturing her lips with mine again.

Her hips rocked into my touch as I delved into the very core of her. She murmured something into our kiss, and I drew away, asking, "Yes?"

Her eyes dragged open, her gaze heavy-lidded as she stared at me. "I don't know, I think I said your name."

I teased my thumb over her clit, watching as her teeth sank into her bottom lip and she let out a little whimper of pleasure when her hips rocked into my touch. Fuck, watching Cammi experience pleasure like this, so raw, so unvarnished, was its own form of torture. I could feel the teeth of my zipper pressing against my cock.

That was going to have to wait. I would eventually experience all of Cammi, but not here, in a hasty fuck in her coffee truck.

"Come for me," I murmured as I drew my fingers out and buried them inside of her again. "Tell me what you need."

She let out a frustrated gasp. "More," she finally said, her tone a little bossy.

I fucked her with my fingers slowly before teasing over her swollen button of need. "That, more of that," she gasped.

I could feel her body tightening as her channel rippled around my fingers, so I kept on going, drawing them out and sinking them in as I stretched her and teased over her clit. One of her hands curled on the edge of the counter, and she gripped it tightly as her body arched like a bow. She let out a long moan and gasped my name in a ragged cry.

I waited until the tremors running through her body stopped. I slowly drew my fingers away and pulled her panties back in place. Conveniently, there was a sink right beside us. I needed to taste her first before I washed it away. Lifting my fingers, I sucked them in my mouth just as Cammi opened her eyes.

Her mouth parted again, her eyes still dark. Her little coffee truck was quiet, save for the sound of her rough breathing as it slowed. Meanwhile, my body felt like a race car, the engine revving and revving. But I wasn't going to let it loose, not tonight.

A sense of fierce tenderness squeezed my heart as I stared at her. This girl had had me since the first day I'd ever laid eyes on her. If she knew me, really, I didn't think she would be here right now.

She reached between us, curling her palm over my cock through my jeans. She gave me a bold stroke, and my cock leaped under her touch. "Let me—" she began, her words stopping abruptly when I shook my head.

"Not tonight. I don't wanna be too greedy."

She looked confused for a minute, so I let my hand trail through the ends of her hair, sliding around to her cheek. "The first time I'm inside of you, it won't be here in your coffee truck."

Her eyes searched mine. "I think I'm the greedy one, but is there something wrong with my coffee truck?"

Chapter Ten

CAMMI

Elias's dark eyes searched mine as he shook his head slowly. "To the contrary, I love your coffee truck. And we should christen it, just not the first time."

The implication that there would be more sent butterflies spinning madly in my belly. Although Elias had just given me a rather spectacular orgasm and I should've been sated, he was so hot that I already wanted more.

I was in a daze as he helped me off the counter and smoothed my skirt down over my hips. This version of Elias was nothing like I expected.

He'd been coming to get coffee from me for years. He was always polite and tipped on the extravagant side, but he wasn't a man of many words, and he held himself back with an edge of grumpy. I'd actually assumed he didn't like me. I was still marveling at him saying he'd wanted me since he met me.

Tonight, he was solicitous, if still quiet. He waited while I made sure everything was put away, taking his coffee with a warm smile. He drove me home and insisted on walking me to my door, which I thought was kind of ridiculous.

I walked in moments later after he had laid another devouring kiss on me. I leaned against the door after I closed it, pressing two fingers over my mouth as if I could hold his kiss there. It felt as if tiny fireworks were exploding in my body.

I listened to the sound of his tires on the gravel as he drove away and wondered when I might see him again. He'd insisted on putting my number in his phone, telling me he'd call me soon.

My night had been weird, to say the least. Dinner with my friends had been nice, but it had all been ruined when I ran into Brad, excuse me, Joel, and his wife. And my tire! Someone slashed my tire. I couldn't help but wonder if it had something to do with Joel and Fran, but that seemed crazy. I needed to get over the fact that I couldn't do anything about what his wife thought of me. Whether or not she believed that I'd knowingly had an affair with her husband was something I couldn't do anything about. Bitterness twisted in my chest. I forcefully shoved those thoughts away and went to take a shower, almost reluctant to do so because I hated to wash away the feel of Elias's touch. That man sure knew how to use his hands.

———

The following morning, I hitched a ride in to my coffee truck with a neighbor who delivered newspapers in the early hours. I opened at five in the morning during the summer, so my days started before dawn. I was grateful to be a morning person because I made bank from the fisherman and tourists who were heading out to the harbor to fish all day. They wanted coffee, and they wanted it early. I was the girl to make it happen. I'd always loved being out and about in these hours. The world felt quiet, as if you were in on a secret that nobody else knew, or at least not many people. I loved the sunrise and the feeling of watching the world wake up.

A few hours later, it was going on eight o'clock and I was finally getting a breather from the madness of the morning rush. My line was gone, and I expected a more stately run of customers now until things slowed down around noon.

My back was to the opening of my serving counter while I quickly stacked fresh cups and got out the muffins I'd bought from the ski lodge. I idly stared at them as I lined them up in the small serving case. I hadn't wanted to compete with Misty Mountain Café all these years. Considering that they had a full-service kitchen, the only thing I competed with them on was coffee. I had to admit, I was good at coffee, and I usually beat them on that front.

I made a mental note to talk to Tess and Susie about their ideas for planning the concept of even buying the coffee shop. I heard the sound of tires on gravel and turned a moment later, anticipating my next customer. My eyes landed on Elias climbing out of his truck. I swallowed as my pulse took off like a rocket and my belly executed a flip.

Sweet hell. That man was hot, need-a-fan hot. Susie's comment was stuck in my head, perhaps because it was so apt. He wore faded jeans, so soft the fabric molded over his muscled thighs. He paired that with leather boots and a faded light blue T-shirt that did nothing to hide his muscled chest and shoulders. I noticed that subtle hitch to his gait again, and my heart squeezed slightly.

He was off his crutches, but I knew that ankle break and the complications hadn't been an easy recovery for him. I hoped he wasn't in pain anymore.

The moment he stopped in front of my window, I felt as if fire flashed over my skin. I shivered in the aftermath of the blast of heat. I instantly recalled that I'd come all over his fingers on this very counter where I now held a coffee cup with my hand resting on the cool steel surface.

"Hi," I squeaked.

Elias dipped his head. "Morning. Think you can escape at some point today?"

"Escape?"

He nodded again. "From here. Tire's all taken care of. I wanted to bring your SUV to you, but it seems I can't drive two vehicles at once," he offered with a wry grin.

"You took care of my tire? Already? How'd you do that?"

He laid a ten-dollar bill down on the counter, and my eyes dropped to his hand. Oh man, now I knew what his hands could do. My cheeks were hot as I lifted my eyes again. If he noticed I was having a bit of a moment, he let it slide.

"I took care of your tire already because I'm an early riser. Can I get a coffee?"

I was flustered, so I focused on starting to make his coffee. "I'll take my usual," he added.

My eyes flew to his, and I said. "Oh! I didn't ask. Although, you've never wanted anything other than your usual once I figured out what it was."

His lips kicked up in a grin, and it felt special, like

a little gift I wanted to reach for and hold in my hand. "True."

As I got his coffee ready, I commented, "You didn't have to fix my tire. Obviously, I appreciate it. I doubt you'll ever need me to fix a tire for you, but if there's anything else I can do, just say so." I handed him his coffee. "You don't need to pay me."

"Yes, I do," he said flatly. We had a little stare off, and then he stuffed the ten-dollar bill in my tip jar and took a swallow of his coffee. "Amazing." He lowered his cup. "Daphne sent me off with a to-go cup from the resort this morning, but her coffee's not as good as yours."

"Coffee is kind of my expertise."

"It is."

We were quiet for a few minutes as he sipped his coffee and blessedly no one else had showed up yet. That wasn't too unusual. The harbor work schedule was definitely early. After the first morning rush, there was a lull, and then it picked up again for the stragglers.

"Actually, I do have a favor you could return," he said.

"Anything," I replied quickly.

He cocked his head to the side, one brow rising as he eyed me. "Anything? Be careful what you promise."

I rolled my eyes. "What is it?"

Elias's lips twisted to the side, and he looked a little sheepish. "Daphne's doing a fundraiser in a few weeks. She's working with Tess on it, and it's turned into this big deal."

"What's it for?"

"She's raising money for a national program for children with rare diseases. If you didn't know, her son died from a rare brain cancer."

I nodded, a shaft of sadness striking me. "I'd heard that. It's so sad."

He nodded. "It is, but she doesn't like to dwell, so this fundraiser is a passion project for her. Long story short, she wants us all there. I was wondering if you'd come with me."

I was so shocked, my mouth fell open.

He almost looked worried. "Is that asking too much?"

I scrambled myself together. I was only shocked because he asked. "Absolutely not. Of course, I'll go. Where is it?"

"At some place up in Kenai. I should know, but I'm just following directions."

"I'll go."

Elias took another swallow of his coffee. "Awesome." He glanced at his watch. "I gotta get out to the airport. I'm tagging along with Diego for a flight. First time I get to fly in months." A slight smile curled his lips.

"Oh, that's awesome!" I clapped my hands lightly and saw the old Elias pop out. He rolled his eyes. "It's not that exciting. It's just my regular job."

"Yeah, but you were in a plane crash, you could've died, and your ankle got all messed up. It's exciting to be able to return to your regular job. I don't care if you're not excited, I am."

Turning, I reached for a cranberry orange muffin, which I knew was one of his favorites. Handing it over, I added, "For good luck. So, will you text me the details for the fundraiser?"

"I need to take you up to get your SUV," he reminded me. "I'll be back from this trip around one. Will you have anybody here then? I can take you right up."

For a moment, I was going to say I could find someone else, but that was just because I was feeling overwhelmed with all of this. Elias had been beyond nice about helping with my tire, and it seemed rude to dismiss his help.

"That'll work. I'll make sure I've got help this afternoon. I think I already have it lined up, but sometimes I lose track."

He held my gaze, just long enough that my pulse raced and my breath got shallow all over again. "I'll see you then."

I might've stared at his mighty fine ass as he walked away, only managing to tear my eyes free when two cars pulled into the parking lot.

Chapter Eleven

ELIAS

A sense of peace rolled through me as I leveled the small plane in the air once we reached cruising altitude. Cruising altitude in a small two-seater plane was very different from that of larger planes that criss-crossed the skies. At this height, the mountains with the waters of Kachemak Bay glittering under the sun below us were close enough it felt almost as if you could reach out and touch them.

"Damn, it feels good to be flying again," I commented into my headset.

Glancing to the side, I caught Diego flashing me a quick grin. "I bet it does. How's your ankle feeling?"

At the moment, my ankle was resting on the floorboard. I flexed it, giving it a careful rotation. "Not one hundred percent, but definitely good enough to be flying."

"Good," he said firmly. "I can't imagine going that long without being in the air."

"Not as bad as it was the last time," I replied.

"I suppose not. I forget you were grounded for six

months before." He was quiet for a moment before adding, "Any pain leftover?"

I shrugged. "Little bit. I'm guessing I'll be able to predict the weather with this ankle for the rest of my life, but nothing that ibuprofen can't knock back." A thread of tension tightened across my shoulders, and I shifted them against the seat.

My last bout with recovery hadn't been a plane crash. Well, except for the fact that a friend of ours— Greg—had been in the crash. I'd been on the crew that responded to help. While we'd been working, there'd been a gas explosion. It hadn't injured me in a life-threatening way, but I got some serious burns where the fabric on the back of my shirt caught fire. Burn pain is like nothing else. They gave me pain meds. Good shit was what that stuff was. Inside of a few weeks, my body wanted more. The emotional aftereffects of my survivor's guilt because Greg didn't make it and I did, made me love the pillowy numbness those painkillers offered.

Not many people knew about that brief episode in my life, except Diego, Flynn, Tucker, and Gabriel. Almost every single fucking person that I worked with now. God, I fucking loved those guys, but I occasionally hated how they checked in with me about pain.

"You're not asking, but there's nothing to worry about. I haven't had cravings in over five years. Fortunately, the doctors here didn't even try to give me that shit."

When I stole a glance of Diego again, he was looking ahead. As if he felt my eyes on him, his gaze slid sideways. "I wasn't worried about you, or that."

My skin felt itchy with annoyance. I hated my own hypersensitivity about my brief tumble into addiction. "Fine," I grumbled.

Diego chuckled. "You *are* fine. Now, pick up the pace. The wind's down, and the sun's out. That's unicorn weather in these parts."

I chuckled, adjusting the speed. We flew along the edge of the bay, making stops in three villages to deliver mail and groceries. When Flynn texted me about coming out to Alaska to work for him, I hadn't realized how much I would love it. Oh, I loved flying, that was practically as vital to my sanity as breathing, but the beauty was breathtaking and a balm to my soul. I also loved the remoteness of some of the places we went. We were greeted by children and anybody who happened to be around—people driving four-wheelers loaded up with groceries to deliver them to the small stores in these far-flung communities. We weren't a passenger service, at least not for these trips. We mostly flew tourists for crazy money and made deliveries. Here and there, if we had room, we'd pick up somebody in a pinch. Today, we scooped up an elderly woman and her niece for a doctor's appointment because she missed one of the regular flights earlier.

"How are you doing today, Marge?" Diego called over his shoulder once we were up in the air. "Haven't seen you in a few weeks."

Marge's dark brown eyes crinkled at the corners in her weathered face as she beamed at Diego. "I've been too busy helping Shana with her new café."

"Café?" Diego prompted.

I had a good view of both of them in the mirror we had mounted up front. We didn't need it like a car driver did, but it was handy for conversation.

Both Marge and Shana had their hair pulled back in a ponytail. Marge's dark hair was streaked with silver. Shana had blue eyes to her grandmother's brown, but otherwise, it was clear as day they were related. They looked so much alike, and their smiles were identical.

Shana grinned. "I started a coffee shop at the back of our grocery store. We're not as high end as Red Truck Coffee, but Cammi gave me all her pointers, so it keeps us busy."

"Making money too," Marge added.

"If your coffee is even close to Cammi's, you'll be making money for years to come," Diego offered.

Of course, there could be no mention of Cammi without my mind spinning back to the feel of my fingers buried inside of her and her body shuddering with her release. Fuck me. Cammi had ruined me.

We lapsed into easy conversation, chatting about the early rush of tourists that would clog up the roads, and the weather, because the weather could be discussed at any time, and how messy mud season was.

After we landed and waved goodbye to Marge and Shana, Diego and I did the usual engine checks on the plane, and then crossed over to our trucks. "You headed straight back?" he asked with his hand resting on the side of his truck.

"Nah, I'm gonna swing by and pick up Cammi to bring her up to her SUV. She had a flat tire last night, and I changed it this morning," I offered, knowing that was only going to be fodder for questions.

Diego's brows hitched up. His eyes took on a gleam as one side of his mouth kicked up in a sly grin. "Nice of you to take care of that for her."

I rolled my eyes. "You'd have done the same thing."

He dipped his head in acknowledgment. "True." He offered nothing further and simply lifted his hand in a quick wave before he climbed in his truck and drove away.

I knew that wouldn't be the last of his comments about Cammi. Especially now that I'd gone and invited her to the fundraiser. It was crazy really, and I didn't care. Even though I should've cared.

———

A few minutes later, I pocketed my keys and approached Red Truck Coffee. It was mid-afternoon, and there was a line. No surprise there. Cammi was busy making coffee, while another woman who looked to be just out of high school was rapidly taking orders. Seeing as I could use a coffee, I got in line.

I took the moment while I waited to look around. The sky was still clear with a soft breeze coming off the bay. Otter Cove Harbor was visible from here. The small cove was tucked off the main bay with low rock cliffs at the base of the mountains on one side and leveling out to a rocky, gray sandy beach on the other.

Boats were starting to stream in from a day of fishing. The wind was picking up slightly from this morning, ruffling the surface of the bay in the distance. I still marveled that I lived somewhere where I could enjoy two things I loved, the ocean and the mountains.

I was a military brat and had grown up with my dad in the Air Force. Our family bounced all over the place until my dad died while on duty. I still missed him. My family stayed where he'd been stationed at the time for a while, and then we moved to where my mom's parents lived in western Oregon. I loved the mountains there. I'd fallen in love with the ocean when we lived near the beach in Texas once.

The views in Alaska were so fucking beautiful they took my breath away. Nature was such a show off sometimes, and I loved it. I heard the screech of an eagle, followed by the loud chatter of a crow. I looked up in the sky to see a fearless crow harassing an eagle in the air. The size differential between the two birds was remarkable, but the crow was relentless and eventually chased the eagle off, perhaps due to sheer annoyance, but it was still effective. A moment later I realized what the crow was after when it flew down to land by a discarded sandwich at the edge of the parking lot.

"You're up," someone said from behind me.

I stepped forward to find Cammi's employee smiling at me politely. She had a fresh face and a tomboyish vibe with her dark hair short, like Cammi's used to be when I first started coming here. "What can I get for you?" she chirped.

Cammi happened to look up right then, and a lightning bolt of awareness struck me, sizzling straight to my balls. A wash of pink crested on her cheeks as we stared at each other for a moment. She snapped out of it first, commenting, "I've got it. Elias always wants a triple shot Americano."

Her helper smiled cheerfully. "Okay, that'll be three-fifty."

I handed over a ten-dollar bill, replying, "Keep the change."

"Give him some freaking change," Cammi added as her eyes bounced to the cash I handed over.

The girl looked uncertain. "Just because," I added, "don't give me any change."

"Amy, give him some change," Cammi said firmly, as she prepped my coffee.

She cast a quick glare in my direction, her cheeks going a little pinker. I suddenly recalled just what we'd been doing on the very counter where she was serving me.

I dropped the silly argument about change. "Okay, fine. Give me three dollars change."

Cammi made a funny little sound, but she said nothing further.

I stepped to the side as the next person began ordering and rested my elbows on the edge of the serving window. "Will you be ready to go soon?" I asked, keeping my voice low.

She looked up and awareness sizzled in the air between us. "Give me fifteen minutes? If that's too much trouble, I can get a friend to take me up there. It's busy, and I don't wanna leave Amy alone yet."

"Fifteen minutes is fine," I assured her. "I need to get some gas anyway. I'll go do that and come back. Okay?"

"You sure?" She handed me my coffee, and our fingers brushed as I took the cup from her. Fire chased over the surface of my skin from that subtle touch.

"I'm sure," I said before stepping away just as Amy called over, "A chai latte, and a latte with an extra shot and caramel syrup, two pumps."

Cammi cast me an apologetic smile, but I lifted my fingers in a wave as I turned and strode back to my truck.

Chapter Twelve

CAMMI

"Thanks again for taking care of my tire," I said for probably the twentieth time today.

Elias looked quickly in my direction before his eyes shifted back to the road in front of us. "It's really no trouble."

I almost said thank you again, but I actually managed to shut my mouth by biting the insides of my cheeks. "Did you have a good flight?" I asked after a moment.

"Sure did. Pretty day for a flight."

"Are you back to your regular schedule?"

"Should be by next week. Gotta say, I'm relieved to be back in the air. It's been a long few months. I'm just grateful my injury happened over the winter when things are slower anyway. Flynn would've been in a bind if the accident had happened during our busy season."

"He would've figured it out. But yeah, I'm sure you're relieved. I hate having time on my hands."

"You have no idea," Elias said firmly, just as the computerized dashboard lit up in front of him with a phone call. The sound of it filled his truck. He glanced at the dashboard screen quickly before casting me an apologetic look. "That's my sister, I'm gonna need to take this."

"Go ahead."

He tapped a button on the screen, answering with, "Hey sis, you're on speaker, and I've got a passenger in the truck."

"Hey, who's riding with you? Is it Diego? Because he owes me five dollars," his sister said.

He chuckled. "No, it's not. You can't see her, but my passenger is Cammi. She runs Red Truck Coffee. I took you there last summer when you came to visit," he replied.

His eyes bounced to mine briefly. "Cammi, this is my sister, Faith."

"Hi, Faith. Elias is just giving me a ride. Sorry to eavesdrop on your conversation."

Faith let out a quick laugh. "I don't think it counts as eavesdropping when Elias put the call on speaker, but that's okay. Nice to meet you."

"What does Diego owe you five bucks for?" Elias prompted.

"We bet on a basketball game. My team won."

"He's ignoring my texts," Faith explained.

Elias chuckled. "Smart man. I'll get the five bucks from him, don't you worry. Now what's up?"

"Mom is driving me crazy. You know how the doctor told her she needs to take it easy? Well, she's not taking it easy. She is still working full-time even though they told her she could cut her schedule back. Will you call her?"

He let out a sigh. "Yeah, I'll call her. What makes you think she's gonna listen to me?"

"Because she always listens to you better than me,"

Faith returned.

"I'm not sure I agree, but I'll definitely call. You doing okay?"

"Of course. I'm always okay." Faith added, "Cammi, Elias is an obnoxious older brother. He's always worried about us when he doesn't need to be."

"Okay, this phone call is over," he interjected with a dry laugh.

"Love you," Faith said quickly.

"Love you too. I'll call mom soon."

He tapped the screen to end the call. "That's my sister. You might not remember, but I did bring her by last summer with my mother and my other sister."

I riffled through my memory. "I think I remember. You stop by a lot with people when you guys are taking tourists around, so I'm not sure. It's hard to keep track. I wouldn't know her if I saw her."

"I wouldn't expect you to have everybody memorized. They'll be here this summer again, so you can rest assured I'll be bringing them by."

"Good to know I count as a stop when you have family."

Elias's eyes slid to mine again, and the heat there sent butterflies twirling in circles in my belly. Dear God. *This* man.

A few minutes later, he pulled up beside my SUV at the ski lodge. With it being late afternoon, the parking lot wasn't as full as it would be when dinner rolled around. Ever since the family who owned this lodge had it renovated, this place was hopping.

I glanced over to see a shiny new tire in place of the one that had been deflated last night. "What did you do with my old tire?" I asked as I climbed out.

"Dropped it off at the transfer station. You must've gotten a new set of tires recently because the treads aren't too worn. You'll want to stop by a mechanic and get your tires rebalanced soon though," he offered. "I also put a spare in the back."

"Elias," I began as I looked up at him. I suddenly realized we were standing mighty close between his truck and my SUV. My pulse skittered off.

"Let's not argue about that. Everybody needs a good spare," he said.

"Let me pay you," I started, moving to open my purse.

He reached out, curling his hand over my wrist. His touch was warm and firm and my pulse went absolutely insane then, my heart kicking against my ribs and butterflies going wild in my belly.

"It's no big deal, okay," he said, his tone easy.

I tried to take a breath, but my lungs were pretty useless. The moment felt hazy and hot. Before I'd quite absorbed what was happening, he stepped closer and dipped his head, brushing his lips across mine briefly.

Just that and nothing more, and my entire body felt electrified and shimmering with heat. I stared blankly up at him, trying to gather my scattered brain cells.

"I'll text you about the fundraiser, okay?" Apparently, he hadn't lost the ability to think and form words.

After too long of a pause, I managed two whole syllables. "Okay." He stood there waiting, looking at me expectantly. "What?" I prompted.

"I was waiting until you got in," he said, gesturing towards my driver's side door.

"Oh!" I was finally galvanized to actually move instead of standing there like a brain-fogged, foolish girl. I climbed in my SUV and started it. I rolled down my window, calling once more, "Thank you. For both rides and for fixing my tire."

He simply dipped his chin and then got in his truck, waiting until I drove away first.

Chapter Thirteen

ELIAS

Two weeks later

The days passed in a blur once I started flying again. It was a relief because time had slowed to a crawl while I'd been healing. Although I saw Cammi every day, like before, now I knew what her lips tasted like underneath mine and precisely how she felt when she flew apart. There was usually a line when I stopped by, as had always been the case. Except now, I felt impatient about it because I wanted to steal a few minutes alone with her.

Flynn assigned me two overnight trips, which I usually jumped at. In a first, I was reluctant, but I took them anyway. I missed Cammi's smile every morning while I was gone more than her coffee.

One evening, I sat at the counter in the kitchen at the resort, my feet hooked on the rung of the stool. "Smells freaking amazing," I said before taking a long pull from my beer.

Daphne was busy cooking something incredibly

fragrant. Her auburn hair was pulled into a tidy braid twisted on top of her head. Her green eyes twinkled with her smile as she looked up quickly, still stirring whatever she had going in the pan with one hand and adjusting the heat on a burner beside it. "I sure hope so. I aim to please."

I chuckled. "Daphne, you're the best cook this place has ever had. It's not even close. You do more than please. The only thing keeping us all from just sitting here like dogs waiting for treats is we're too busy."

"Are you already complaining about the schedule?" Flynn asked as he approached from where he'd been standing over by the table in the front of the room. He slipped his hips onto the stool beside me.

"Hell no, I'm not complaining. Just telling Daphne that's the only reason we're all not trapped here in the kitchen waiting for what she makes next."

Flynn cuffed me lightly on the shoulder as he laughed. When he looked over at Daphne, his smile stayed, but the intensity in his eyes shifted. Flynn had fallen so hard for Daphne, it was still a little startling. I wasn't much for romance, but even I had to admit they seemed perfect for each other. Prim and proper as Daphne could come across, the woman was strong with a streak of sass and could stand up to Flynn's tendency to be a cranky ass.

"What are you making?" he asked.

"Seasoned rice with sautéed veggies. I'm baking some halibut with a light lemon sauce. It's all gonna be good."

My mouth started watering then. Daphne was already dashing to the opposite side of the kitchen to fetch some spices. Flynn stood and crossed over to the pantry. Of course, because he was whipped, he stopped beside her and pressed a lingering kiss on the side of her neck. When he paused in the doorway of the large pantry, he glanced to me again. "Need another one?" He lifted his chin toward the beer in my hand.

"Nah. Just got this one a few minutes ago."

"I'll take one," Diego's voice came over my shoulder.

Glancing back, I saw him coming into the kitchen through the archway that led into the main guest area of the resort. On his heels were Tucker and Nora. Tucker had also flown with us in the Air Force, and Nora was Flynn's younger sister. Right behind them came Grant, Flynn's younger brother, and then last, but definitely not least, came Cat, the youngest of the four siblings. Cat was still in high school and lived here in the family's private apartment with Flynn and Daphne.

I called over to the pantry. "Might want to grab enough for—" I took a quick head count. "Four more."

"Me too," Cat called.

Flynn came out of the pantry with a six-pack from the local brewery in his hand. He cast a quick look at Cat. "Hell no."

Cat gave him an impish smile. In a minute, the counter was crowded. Everybody except Cat pulled up a stool and sat down. Cat hurried through the door into the family's apartment. Daphne looked up with a smile. "Oh, I got a full kitchen tonight."

"You always have a full kitchen," Nora said solemnly.

Daphne grinned. "Actually, not always when we don't have guests."

This was a rare weekend when the resort wasn't booked. Flynn had wanted to do some work on the roof, so we'd all be doing that this weekend. He hadn't scheduled any bookings so we didn't have to stress about guests meandering under ladders while we did the work.

Nora shook her head. "Daphne, this is the first time since you've been here that we don't have any guests. We'd have been nuts not to take advantage of it. For once, we don't have to be polite and make sure we don't run out of whatever you're making. It's every-woman for herself tonight," Nora said, casting a daring glance amongst us as she waggled her eyebrows.

Of the Walker siblings, Nora was the only one who didn't share Flynn's coloring of dark blond hair and ice blue eyes. She had rich brown hair with eyes to match. She was beautiful, and for probably the one-thousandth time, I thanked God she did nothing for me. On the other hand, Gabriel and her had so much sexual tension between them, they were like two fighting cats most of the time. So far, they'd managed to keep a lid on it.

Cat skipped around the counter to stand beside Daphne after reappearing in the kitchen. "What can I help with?"

"Can you check on the halibut for me? If you don't mind," Daphne replied.

"Course I don't mind," Cat said. "That's why I asked."

Flynn was systematically opening beers and passing them to the rest of the group. "I'm gonna need to start paying you," he called over to Cat.

"Exactly," she returned as she opened the oven.

Daphne looked up at Flynn when she set a cover over the large wok pan where the rice was and turned off the burner underneath. "You really should pay her. She helps me a lot."

When Cat returned, inspecting what Daphne was doing, Flynn added, "We'll make it official and put you on the payroll. You need to fill out some paperwork though."

"Paperwork?" Cat queried.

"Yup. In Alaska if you want to work when you're sixteen, we have to apply for a work permit for you, and I have to consent to you getting the job. It's a liability issue."

"Can't you pay me under the table?" Cat asked, all nonchalant.

Grant let out a laugh at that. "Jesus. She's already negotiating."

Flynn merely rolled his eyes, taking it in stride. "Nothing under the table. We're all official here."

Cat let out an aggrieved sigh as Flynn chuckled. "We'll do the paperwork together. Pretty sure it's no big deal."

We settled in for a rare night here where it was just staff. Flynn couldn't have known how much I needed this job when he'd reached out. I had just finished my time in the Air Force and was on the other side of my short-lived but brutal episode of opiate addiction. With my own experience and tracking the news, I was convinced those damn pills were evil, as were the pharmaceutical companies that lied through their teeth for years while they made money hand over fist. Coming to Alaska and being able to do what I loved and be with guys who were like brothers to me helped me re-center and catch my balance in the never-ending ride of life.

Later that night, I let my eyes travel around our hodgepodge group. We had decamped from the counter over to the main table, a large rectangular table situated in front of windows that ran the length of the room. The windows offered a view of the field outside the resort with the hills rolling downward to reveal the mountains and ocean in the distance. The sun was being extravagant tonight as it set with the sky awash in pink, purple, and the fading gold of the sun's rays lingering through the colors.

Nora was at one end of the table helping Cat with her math homework. Flynn, looking more relaxed than usual, leaned back in his chair with his arm draped over Daphne's shoulders. Diego was sitting beside me, debating the finer points of dipnetting with Tucker and Gabriel. He glanced to me for assistance. "Don't you think it's better when you make the pole with cedar so it floats?"

"Agreed," I said quickly.

Gabriel narrowed his eyes. "Really? You're limited with shape when you use cedar for the pole. All you can do is make a square or rectangle net. I like the metal or the stainless steel because I can make it into a big loop."

"What do you think?" I prompted, lifting my chin toward Tucker who sat across from me.

Tucker, ever affable, simply shrugged. "Whatever works for y'all."

Grant had left the room to go to the bathroom and returned, sitting down beside Tucker. "What do you think?" Tucker asked him.

Grant looked amongst us. "Uh, what are we talking about?"

"The finer points of dipnetting," I offered as I chuckled.

Dipnetting was a beloved Alaska tradition. You had to wait until you were a resident for a full year to even consider it. During short periods of time in fish season, residents could show up and stick a net in the water and catch salmon. It was like nothing I'd ever seen and a total blast.

"Cedar," Grant said firmly, getting into the swing of the conversation immediately.

Grant was younger than Flynn by five years. He was more easy-going than Flynn, but was otherwise so much like him it was amusing at times. He was ever practical and quick. He was also shaping up to be a great pilot. I'd been one of his instructors for his training hours

Flynn, picking up on our conversation, called over, "Cedar."

Gabriel rolled his eyes. "Fine. I'll just have the best-looking net."

Nora glanced up. "Who cares how the net looks?"

"And, here we go," Diego muttered under his breath.

I grinned. "It won't last long. They usually don't argue too much when Flynn is around."

Daphne cut the debate off at the pass. She tapped her hand lightly on the table. "While we're all here, can we chat about the fundraiser coming up?"

"We will all be there," Diego said, putting his palm over his chest and giving her a solemn nod.

"We'll also be on our best behavior," Tucker added.

"I would expect nothing less," Daphne said in her precise, slightly Southern accent. "I just want to thank y'all for supporting this. It means a lot to me."

Nora chimed in, "Of course we support it. I think you should do a fundraiser every year."

"Maybe," Daphne replied lightly. "It's turned out to be a lot of work, and that's with Tess helping me."

She was referring to Tess Winters, who was a bigwig fundraiser. She moved to Diamond Creek some years ago after she met a mutual friend of ours,

Nathan Winters. Ever since Tess moved to town, Diamond Creek and other nearby communities had more conferences and events than ever before because Tess organized them.

Flynn was always trying to spread the word about the resort, so he signed us up for pretty much everything. That was my only complaint about this job because he often prevailed upon us to attend events with him.

"Please God, tell me you don't expect us to wear a suit," Gabriel commented.

"You don't have to wear a suit," Daphne said in a soothing tone. "You could look nice. There probably will be people there in suits. It won't kill you to at least shower and maybe shave."

Diego scrubbed his hand along his chin, which had several days of stubble growing. "I'll shave, I promise. I probably won't wear a tie, but I'll wear a button down. Also, Elias is bringing a date."

Fuck my life. I should've known Diego was waiting for the right moment to tease me about Cammi.

I slid a look at him. "Really?"

Cat straightened in her chair, her curious eyes bearing down on me. "Who?"

I rolled my eyes.

"Well, we're all going to meet the mystery girl next weekend," Nora chimed in from Cat's side as she set down her pencil.

"True. I invited Cammi."

"From Red Truck Coffee?" Daphne prompted.

I finished off my beer and nodded. "She's the only Cammi I know."

"Oh, I like her. I can't believe she's coming with you," Cat added, her tone bordering on incredulous.

"I wasn't looking for your personal approval, but thank you."

Flynn caught my eye, a knowing glint in his. He'd been giving me a little hell about Cammi for some time. I didn't want to prove him right, but the temptation of her was too much for me to go out of my way to prove him wrong. "Okay, now everybody knows. Can we stop talking about it now?"

"You'd better be nice to her," Cat said, her eyes narrowing almost comically.

"I'm not known for being an asshole to women," I returned.

Cat wrinkled her nose and pursed her lips as she stared at me. "Maybe not an asshole specifically, but you and Flynn could have a contest for cranky."

Grant burst out laughing, along with Diego.

"Although, Flynn's been much better since Daphne got here. Maybe you'll be nicer if you get a girlfriend," Cat added matter of factly.

Even I couldn't help but laugh at that.

Chapter Fourteen

ELIAS

Hours later, I found myself unable to sleep, which was nothing new. Sleep and I had never gotten along all that well. The regimented routine of the military had helped somewhat, but then everything blew to smithereens when Greg died. I got hurt and then got hooked on those asinine pills.

Since then, I felt like I was in an endless boxing match with sleep. I was gradually coming to peace with the fact that sometimes I'd wake up and need to get out of bed to snap my brain out of its habit of rummaging around in the dark, casting about for every painful regret or needless worry I could find.

I walked outside in the darkness after shrugging into my jacket and lowered my hips onto the top step. Just last month, all of us had finally finished building a house a stone's throw away from the main resort building. It was nice too. There were six bedrooms in here and four showers, along with a nice hangout space downstairs and an efficiency kitchen. We'd been working on it in fits and starts over the last year or more and took the winter months to get the interior complete for us to move in. With my limited mobility over the winter, I hadn't been able to do as much as I'd wanted, but I'd managed to help some.

I stayed here with Diego, Tucker, Gabriel and Grant. Nora had her own place nearby, while Flynn and Cat lived at the main building with Daphne. I was relieved to be able to get around without my crutches and not need to stay in the room there anymore.

I rested my chin on my two fists stacked on top of each other and stared out into the darkness. A barred owl hooted nearby, and I heard a rustling in the trees. It was loud enough that I figured it was a squirrel. Small animals generally made the most noise in the woods.

My mind spun to the call I'd made to my mother recently, as I'd promised my sister. My mom wasn't adjusting to aging all that well. She'd always been active and hated slowing down. It didn't help that she was a medical assistant, and there was always work to be had at the local hospital where she'd worked for years. She had rheumatoid arthritis and wasn't too pleased with how stress exacerbated it. She'd told me she knew she needed to scale back and promised she'd already talked to the hospital about it. Of course, she only got to that after I pointed out how I'd hate to see her lose more mobility by pushing herself too hard.

I was tight with my mom and my sisters. If I was ever going to move away from here, they would be the only reason why. It's just that there was peace here in Alaska, and I needed that right now. Oregon was close enough for me to fly there in half a day, so I tried to take care of them from a distance.

I took a deep breath, my lungs filling with the crisp, early spring air. My breath misted as I let it out. My thoughts had been chasing each other when I couldn't sleep, mostly getting hung up on Cammi. But then, I couldn't blame Cammi for my lack of sleep. Hell, she'd pitched a tent in every corner of my thoughts whether I was awake or asleep.

I'd known I was feathering along the edges of a bad decision when I gave in and kissed her. Not because I didn't want to kiss her. Not because she wasn't sexy, sweet, a little sassy, and more emotionally fragile than I wanted to contemplate. No, rather, the problem was me. Once in my life, I'd slipped, not even for that long, but it had thrown my entire perception of myself and my ability to keep my shit together into disarray ever since.

I heard footsteps approaching, the subtle crunch of one boot after another landing on the ground. Although there was still snow left at the higher elevations, there wasn't much on the well-worn path between the main resort and our staff house, or as Diego dubbed it, 'the guy place'.

In a moment, the shadow of a man appeared, and I knew immediately it was Diego. Even in the dark, I'd recognize any of the guys I worked with here. We all knew each other too well. Diego was the tallest of all of us and had an easy, rangy stride.

He stopped in front of the steps, and our eyes were practically level with him standing and me sitting on the top step. "What the hell are you doing out here?" he asked.

"The better question would be what the hell are you doing out at this hour?" I countered.

Diego shrugged easily. "I went into town for a bit after dinner. Needed to see some other faces. You doing okay?" He climbed the steps and rested his hips beside mine to look out into the darkness.

"I'm okay. Wasn't sleeping well."

"How's your pain?"

Diego knew me better than probably any of the guys here, and we all knew each other well. It's just he was fucking perceptive as hell. He was solid as they came too. He had a philosophical bent that could be at odds with his intense loyalty and emotional nature.

I knew he was only asking because he was concerned, but every time somebody asked me about my pain, it felt as if my nerve endings were too raw to even tolerate the question. It was like a mosquito in the darkness that you wanted to swat—fucking annoying as hell and impossible to find.

I took a breath and let it out again. It was too cold for mosquitoes now. "It's fine. Annoying, but what are you gonna do?"

"Not much, I suppose. How was your flight today?"

"Fucking awesome."

Diego chuckled. He leaned sideways, nudging me with his shoulder. "Damn glad you're in the air again."

"Did you have to bring up Cammi tonight?" I asked, surprising myself with my question.

He chuckled again. Although I couldn't see his eyes in the darkness, I knew there was a slight gleam contained in them. "Might as well go ahead and face the music. I think Cammi will be good for you."

"Why do you say that?"

"Aside from her world-class coffee, she's a sunny person. You could use a little of that. Plus, you're worth someone like her."

I heard Diego's words, but it felt as if my own doubts were charging at me, ready to trample over his voice. He said it with such faith.

Chapter Fifteen

CAMMI

I was zooming through a busy morning at the coffee truck. My thoughts were split between wondering when Elias might stop by, my plan to meet at the bank with Susie today to discuss a proposal to purchase Misty Mountain Café, and the text I'd received only moments ago. Truth be told, the text was occupying all my thoughts right now. I just didn't like admitting it.

Sorry about your tire. Fran knew it was your SUV. I'd love to see you. I'm really sorry about the way everything went down. I never should've lied to you.

Stupid fucking lying Brad-slash-Joel. Of course, I had blocked the number I knew to be his, but clearly, he'd either gotten a new number, or signed up for some bullshit burner phone. I contemplated reporting him and his wife to the police for property damage, but it wasn't worth it. It hadn't cost me a penny because Elias was still refusing to let me pay him back. Not to mention the sheer mortification involved in showing up at the police station and filing a report about the man who'd lied and pretended to be somebody he wasn't and who I'd accidentally had an affair with. The very end of that ridiculous story was that his wife apparently stabbed my tire. It was all messy and embarrassing.

Diamond Creek was such a small town that the newspaper printed all police reports every week. The only time they cut them short was during tourist season. They left out names, but people would know. Then, if there were actually charges filed, the names would be in the court reports, which were also printed weekly. Fuck my life. My cheeks got hot simply contemplating the situation.

"Here you go," I said, handing another coffee to Amy. I was faster at making coffees, and she was turning out to be great with customers. She didn't even care when they were rude to her. She just let it roll right off her shoulders. I mostly did too, but she had a sunny, cheerful nature that would serve her well in life until she got cynical.

Just because my morning needed to be more annoying, I then heard Brad's—excuse me—Joel's voice.

For the first time ever, I wished Amy would be a total bitch. She wasn't. Le sigh. She greeted him cheerfully. "Hi there, what can we get for you this morning?"

I kept my head turned away, busy wiping down the espresso machine. The task most definitely needed to be done, so it wasn't idle cleaning.

"I'll just take the house coffee with a shot of hot water added to it," Joel said.

Oh, right. Way back when, I should've known he was an idiot. My house coffee was delicious, but he preferred it weaker than it was. That pretty much said it all. Even his coffee preference was half-assed.

I stole a glance at Amy. She managed to keep smiling, but I could see the hint of horror in her eyes. I almost snorted a laugh and had to bite my cheeks.

"Hi, Cammi," Joel added while Amy was ringing him up.

I glanced up briefly. "Hi."

The second my eyes bounced past Joel, I wanted to disappear and wished I had the power to make it so. Because Elias was pulling into a parking spot. Just my luck. Sure, we could all agree that Joel was a total ass, but it didn't change how idiotic I felt for stumbling into that situation.

There was a family behind Joel, so Elias had to wait. I ignored Joel, even when he stepped over to the side of the window to try to talk. "Did you get my text? I was hoping we could talk."

"Yup, I did, and no, we won't be talking. Please don't text me again."

I actually handed his coffee to Amy to serve him rather than giving it to him myself. He was still there when Elias got to the front of the line. I absolutely couldn't resist lifting my eyes to look at Elias. His shaggy dark blond hair looked windblown, and his eyes were waiting for me. I sensed he recognized Joel from that night in the reception area at the lodge. Even though I was embarrassed because I didn't like being reminded of the biggest mistake I'd ever made—one made worse because it caused other people pain—the moment I met Elias's eyes, I felt protected.

He exuded an unconscious strength that I needed. Seeing him there with Joel only set off the contrast between the two men. Joel was handsome, but everything was only skin deep on him. He ran a seasonal outdoor gear shop, trying to compete with a local business and not doing so great from what I could tell. He wore shiny, new outdoor clothing, a stark contrast to Elias's battered and faded blue jeans and well-worn jacket. Elias was several inches taller with broad shoulders and an easy stance. It was like comparing plastic to steel.

"Hey, Cammi," Elias said.

All of my parts shimmied at the sound of his low, melodic voice. I kind of even forgot Joel was there for a minute. After Elias ordered his usual, which was *way* stronger than Joel's lame coffee, he stepped to the side. His eyes flicked briefly to Joel before looking away dismissively.

"How's it going?" he asked, his attention like a beam of warmth on me.

Joel, being the ass he was, cut in, "I was actually talking with her."

Now, Elias's eyes slid slowly to him. I couldn't quite read the look there, but I sensed a hint of anger and clear dominance.

"No, we weren't," I squeaked.

Elias's lips curled, just barely, at one corner as he looked back toward me. Joel was silent for a few seconds before he turned and walked away.

"Please don't come back," I called.

He glanced over his shoulder, shaking his head as if he was somehow disappointed in me. Maybe I was rude, but good grief, the man had lied his way into an affair with me. He'd set the bar so low I didn't feel like I needed to be polite.

With Joel gone, Elias stepped closer, resting his elbow on the inside of the window. I finished getting his coffee ready and handed it over. "There you go."

Once again, he stuffed way too much money in the tip jar. I wasn't going to argue about that because Amy deserved the tips.

"We're still on for this weekend?" he asked.

As appeared to be the case whenever Elias was close to me, my lungs didn't work too well, and I felt hot all over. I wondered if I was having early menopause, and these were hot flashes. I dismissed that quickly. I wasn't old enough, and this crazy heat was Elias-specific.

"Of course." My voice came out breathy, but what could a girl do when faced with a package of hot, delectable Elias? It was all just too much.

I peered through the serving window at my coffee truck. A storm was rolling in with dark clouds burgeoning in the sky and an icy wind kicking up from the bay. My old baker's truck was sturdy, but it still rattled with the wind when it blew too hard. A stack of my red paper coffee cups toppled to the floor, and I turned to pick them up quickly.

Amy finished taking the last order. I prepped the coffee, glancing to the little red clock mounted above our heads on the inside of the truck. It was early evening, but I doubted anyone else would show, not with the weather blowing in. The parking lot was empty, and there was a steady stream of vehicles passing us by as rain began to fall. A gust of wind blew some icy cold drops into the truck.

"Why don't you go home? I'll close up," I said with a glance in Amy's direction.

"Are you sure?" she asked.

I cast her a quick smile. "I love how you're always willing to stay for your whole shift. We're not gonna get any more customers, and the weather is crap."

As if Amy's mother telepathically read my mind,

she pulled into the parking area and waved from her car. She rolled down her window, calling, "Are you ladies closing up early?"

"Absolutely," I called in return, my voice almost lost in the wind.

While Amy got her jacket and purse, I quickly prepped her mother's favorite coffee to go. I handed it to her. "Give this to your mom."

Amy dashed through the now steady falling rain as I rolled down the steel curtain for the window to lock it from the inside. I felt as if I were in a little cocoon as the wind howled outside. I turned on some seventies music to listen to while I cleaned up.

I was deep into jamming out to a song by the Bee Gees when I felt a particularly rattling gust against my coffee truck and heard a loud thump from a distance outside. Considering that I was safe and sound and dry, I carried on with my cleaning.

Not much later, there was a knock at the back of the coffee truck. Since I knew it was still pouring outside because the rain was pounding on the roof, I had no idea who was crazy enough to stop for coffee now. Thinking it was an errant customer with wishful hopes since my SUV was outside, I opened the door, surprised to find Elias standing there. He had no rain jacket on and his hair was wet. Without thinking, I tugged him inside. "What are you doing? It's awful out."

I was relieved to close the door behind him again and shut out the wind and rain. He was so wet, water dripped onto the steel floor beneath his feet. "I needed a coffee," he opened with.

"I'm happy to make you a coffee, but that's crazy to run through the rain like that. I hope none of you all are up in the air this evening."

I reached for a clean towel from the stack of dish-towels ever-present on the corner of the counter by my espresso maker. He used it to wipe over his hair and dry his face and hands. I turned to get a coffee ready for him.

"All of our planes are on the ground, and I do want coffee, but I stopped because your windshield has a tree limb through it."

"What?" My hands fell away after I automatically tapped the start button for his double shot of espresso.

Elias nodded calmly. "Yep, there's a big tree limb poking right through it."

I leaned my hips against the counter behind me and let out a ragged sigh. "You're kidding."

"Definitely not kidding, and not the kind of thing I would joke about. I figured you might need a ride. I mean, unless you want to drive home with a tree branch as your passenger and rain in your face."

I actually laughed, and I needed it. "Definitely not."

The espresso machine beeped at me, letting me know Elias's shots were ready. I stepped to the side and quickly got his coffee ready before handing it to him.

"I tied a tarp over your windshield. Didn't want it to get too wet inside," he commented.

"Geez, is there anything you don't think of? Thank you so much."

"No worries. I have a few tarps in my truck, so figured it was the best option until you can deal with it."

"Thank you. Really. If you need to get going, I can call a friend for a ride," I offered, thinking Elias had helped me out in a pinch once already.

"I'm here already, and you just made me some awesome coffee," he replied with a quick grin.

"Can you wait for a few minutes? I was just cleaning up in here."

"Rocking out to the Bee Gees, I see," he teased.

"I love the Bee Gees," I said with a true loyalty I felt deep in my soul.

"I'm a fan too," he offered before taking a long swallow of his coffee.

I wiped down the espresso machine again and finished cleaning the sink before putting everything away and grabbing the cash bag and my laptop. When I glanced up toward Elias, he was studying the small chalkboard I had mounted on the inside of the door.

I hadn't updated it lately, but the two phrases jotted there were still worthy.

Don't forget to smile. Bee kind.

There was a bumble bee drawn beside the second phrase.

"Do you change those up very often?" His eyes slid to mine.

In this moment where I wasn't distracted by something else and I was alone with Elias, it felt like little fireworks went off in my body. All my girly parts woke up and that shimmering chemistry hummed to life in the air around us.

I must've stared a few beats too long because he prompted, "Cammi?"

"Oh!" I tore my eyes from his, looking quickly at the chalkboard. "I do sometimes. When the mood strikes me."

"It suits you."

"What suits me?"

"The chalkboard with motivational quotes in different colors. You strike me as the kind of person who wants the world to be a better place. Words matter."

It suddenly felt as if Elias was telling me something more than the sum of his words. As we stared at each other, he looked slightly surprised and amused. "They do," I finally replied.

The coffee truck rattled again with a punishing gust of wind. "Should we go?" I asked.

Oddly, I didn't want to leave. I could've stayed right there in my little truck with Elias looking good enough to eat and dangerous for my sanity. Because I felt safe. I hadn't realized that I hadn't felt safe. Not physical safety, but more that sense of doubting who you're with and what they thought.

After a long moment, he took a swallow of his coffee and nodded. "Let's."

He held the door for me and waited while I made sure to get it locked up with a padlock from the outside on the door and the front window. After we dashed through the rain to his truck, we were both soaked by the time we climbed inside. There was no way to avoid it. My teeth were chattering slightly as I glanced to him. Elias tapped the button to start his truck and put the heat on full blast. "No raincoat?" he asked as his eyes swept over me.

My hair was dripping, just as his was. "You don't have one either," I countered.

He reached behind the seat and handed me a towel. "It's clean."

I rubbed the towel over my hair, neck and face before handing it to him. He did the same. "Let's get you home." He tossed the towel over the seat.

Although we were no longer in my coffee truck, it felt as if there was a little bubble around us. The weather was, as I'd predicted, just awful. When I looked out toward the bay, I could hardly tell the difference between the slate gray surface of the ocean and the rain falling from the sky except for a subtle shade of darker color. Wind buffeted his truck as he drove.

Chapter Sixteen

CAMMI

I let myself steal a glance at him and felt butterflies spiraling in my belly. I was dripping wet, the absolute opposite of sexy. But my body didn't really think about much when it came to Elias. With the chill in the air, he exuded a cool, but easy masculinity that I wanted to wrap around myself.

The drive was quiet, and I bit my tongue several times to keep from thanking him too much. "I don't know what to do about my windshield," I finally said with a frustrated sigh.

"You'll get it fixed. I took a look at it when I tied the tarp down. It's just the glass. It'll be all right. Insurance actually makes it easy to get windshields repaired. If you have a regular mechanic, call them. If you need a suggestion, I can scare up the number of the place we use at the resort."

"I'll call my insurance company tomorrow and go from there. Thanks again." I paused before blurting out. "I seem to be thanking you a lot. I promise I'm not always an accident waiting to happen."

"Shit happens to all of us. I'm sure you'll get to return the favor someday," he replied easily.

"Do you want to get pizza?" I asked impulsively.

He slowed to a stop at the intersection just before he would turn onto the road that led toward my place. His eyes slid to mine. "Darlin', I'll never say no to pizza."

My lips curled into a smile. "Head to Glacier Pizza then. It's on the way."

Moments later, the neon sign for Glacier Pizza loomed through the rain. "My treat," I said when he stopped in the parking lot

He started to protest, but I shook my head firmly. "You fixed my tire for free, gave me a ride home and back the next day, and you had the foresight to put a tarp over my broken windshield. Let me get the pizza. You wait here."

Glacier Pizza was a local and a tourist favorite. I pushed through the door. Although the crowd was thin, there were still a few scattered customers, and it was cozy and warm in here. This was a basic, no frills restaurant with amazing pizza. A massive brick oven sat in the center of the space with an open kitchen and counter encircling it. Customers could watch the pizza process while sitting at the stools by the counter, or relax in the booths lining the walls. There were photos from locals and tourists lining the walls, along with license plates from all over the country.

I hurried over to the counter, asking the young man, Ryan, behind the register, "What large pizzas do you have ready to go?"

That was one of the best things about Glacier Pizza. They kept pizzas ready to sell by the slice or full size. You could order your own choices, but everything they made in their wood-fired oven was delicious.

The guy turned to stride toward the back of the kitchen to check. I quickly texted Elias.

Are you picky? Will pepperoni work? Or are you vegetarian or vegan? I added a wink emoticon after that. Somehow, I seriously doubted Elias was vegetarian, much less vegan.

He replied almost instantly. *I love pepperoni, but I like vegetables too. I'll take whatever they have and whatever you prefer.*

Ryan returned to the counter and cast me a quick smile. "All we've got left is pepperoni and plain cheese. We've had a run on the ready-made stuff."

"I'll take two large pepperonis if you have enough."

A few minutes later as Ryan was ringing me up, I asked, "How are things at the store?" I was referring to the outdoor gear store his older brother Eli owned and where he also worked. Ryan did as many Alaskans did and worked multiple jobs. He picked up hours here, worked for his brother, and was also training to be a hotshot firefighter.

"Not so busy yet, but give it a few weeks and things will start picking up. Winters are our quiet time, which is why I work more here," he replied with a quick smile.

"I'm sure Eli would keep you busy if you wanted more hours," I returned as I put the change in the tip jar by the register.

Ryan gave an easy shrug. "He gives me plenty of hours, but I like money. I work forty hours there and then do three nights here. I'm saving up for a truck."

"You're a good kid."

Ryan cast me a faux glare. "I'm not a kid anymore, Cammi. I'm twenty-one. I can legally drink."

I flashed him a smile. "Okay, okay. You're not a kid, but don't be stupid about alcohol."

He rolled his eyes and waved me off. In the time I'd gotten to know Ryan, mostly through knowing Eli and his wife Jessa, I'd learned he was old for his years. He was reliable and responsible, and I kind of wished maybe he could just be irresponsible for a little bit.

"Stay dry," I called as I left and dashed under the awning into Elias's truck.

He looked at my hands as I set the two boxes of pizza on my lap. "Two boxes?"

"You can never have too much pizza. Plus, leftover pizza for breakfast is the bomb."

Instantly, I realized I wanted to offer leftover breakfast pizza at Misty Mountain Café. It wouldn't be true leftovers, but I could advertise the concept. I reached for my phone and quickly typed the idea into my notes.

I felt Elias's gaze on me and glanced over. "What?"

"I'm not going anywhere until you buckle up. What's so important you need to jot a note down right now? Color me curious."

I suddenly felt a little shy. Only Susie and Tess knew I was actually taking the steps to seriously consider buying the café. But Susie said my numbers looked good, so maybe I had a real shot.

"I had an idea for breakfast. I'm looking into buying Misty Mountain Café because the owners are selling. I'll be able to make a lot more stuff there, and I thought it would be fun to have fake leftover pizza for breakfast. What do you think?"

It was quiet for so long that I started to feel foolish, but then a smile slowly unfurled from one corner of his mouth to the other. "That's fucking genius. Now, buckle up and let's get you home so we can enjoy that pizza."

It felt as if my heart was actually smiling. Elias wasn't the kind of guy to hand out compliments easily. If at all.

Chapter Seventeen

ELIAS

Cammi sat on a stool in her kitchen. She had a cute, maybe even charming, place. It was small, but felt spacious. The space was open with a view of what I presumed was the bay, although we couldn't see a damned thing right now. Nothing but driving rain was visible outside the windows. There was an oval-shaped island separating the living room and kitchen. The living room had a couch and a loveseat that were facing each other with a pair of matching chairs, and a fireplace with the television mounted above it.

She'd insisted on starting a fire when we got here. I dried off as best I could, but my clothes were damp. She returned from what I presumed was her bedroom. She'd changed into a long sleeve T-shirt and a pair of sweatpants. Her hair was drying in messy waves around her shoulders, and her cheeks were still flushed from our dash through the rain into the house. She eyed me, tapping her fingers on the counter.

"Hang on a sec. Susie left a fishing bag here from last summer. It's in the coat closet. I bet there's a clean change of clothes that might fit you."

"Uh, I appreciate it, but I seriously doubt Susie's clothes would fit me," I called over.

She hurried to a closet by the door, coming out beaming. "Here it is. You know Jared, right? I went fishing with him and Susie. I know her clothes won't fit, but I bet his will."

"Of course, I know Jared. We refer clients to them all the time. And, you're right, we are probably close to the same size." I took the bag she handed me and went into the bathroom, relieved to change out of my damp clothes into the borrowed T-shirt and jeans.

Not much later, I took a swallow of beer, Diamond Creek Brewery, of course, before lifting another slice of pizza. "They do make good pizza," I commented after I finished chewing.

Cammi was not one to hold back when it came to eating. She was working on her third slice of pizza. She smiled over at me. "I know. They've been around forever, and they don't need to change a thing. It's just perfect."

She finished her slice with relish before leaning back. "I need to take a food break."

The wind was blowing the rain against the windows, creating a cacophony that sounded like tiny pebbles striking again and again. She pushed her plate away and lifted her wine glass to take a swallow. My eyes snagged on her bottom lip when her tongue darted out to catch a drop of wine at the corner.

Nothing about what was happening with Cammi felt within my control. It was a cascade of events, each one increasing the momentum and shredding my discipline.

The wind came in rolling gusts off the bay, buffeting her small house as the land and the ocean pushed the wind back and forth in the dance of the storm. The lights flickered after a sustained rush of wind. Cammi unhooked her toes from the rungs on her stool and stood, hurrying around the island to open a cabinet above the stove. She pulled out several candles, the thick, chunky kind. She placed two on the counter and then circled the house, distributing a few more.

I went to check on the fire and add a little more wood. If we lost power, we would be toasty as long as we stayed in the living room. When I straightened, she had a lighter in her hand and lit the two candles in the kitchen. She glanced up at me as I approached.

"This way, if the power goes out, there'll be a little light." She paused, her eyes searching mine. "If you're going to go home, you might want to go soon. I know your drive is at least twenty minutes."

If I had any sense, I would've opened my mouth and told her that, yes, I was going home. But I didn't want to leave. Every cell in my body was tuned to the frequency of Cammi, and I needed her. My need for her was unlike any I'd ever experienced. I'd had my share of desire and casual encounters, many hot, quick, and fun.

Yet, with Cammi, there was a sense of burgeoning, my draw to her running deep and anything but casual.

I closed the distance between us, stopping in front of her where she stood with her hips resting against the edge of the counter. She still held the lighter in her hand, and I reached for it, the burn of electricity sizzling up my arm from where my fingers brushed against hers. I set it on the counter before resting my hands on either side of her hips. Her eyes blinked up at me. The subtle hitch of her breath in her throat was like the lash of a whip against my already galloping need.

I closed my eyes for a moment, taking in a swift inhalation of air. Opening my eyes, I finally did what I'd been wanting to do, well, since the last time I kissed her.

Dipping my head, I pressed a kiss on the side of her neck. I already knew she was sensitive there. Another hitch of her breath, and I pressed open kisses along her jawline as I found my way to her mouth.

With licks of heat racing through me, our kiss got hot and heavy. Her sassy tongue twined with mine as I dove into the sweet taste of her mouth. Too soon, I needed air, which was in short supply whenever I was too close to her.

Breaking free, I took in a gulping breath. Her eyes were hazy and dark, and her cheeks flushed. I could feel the press of the zipper teeth against my swollen and aching cock. My thin cotton briefs weren't much help when I needed her this much.

"What are we doing, Elias?"

Her voice was raspy and breathy. I just wanted to kiss her all over again. I simultaneously wanted all of her right now, and yet I didn't want to rush it because then I'd miss all the details.

"Kissing." I paused and took another breath. "And then, whatever comes after that," I added.

She was quiet for a few beats, while the air around us felt loaded, quickening with the energy and spark of our desire. "Okay," she whispered, just before leaning forward and stringing kisses along my collarbone.

Fierce wind lashed the house. The lights flickered, going out and coming back on before going out again.

"Smart move," I murmured.

I gave in to the urge to trail my hand down and cup her breast. Her nipple pebbled under my touch. I was gratified to discover she was not wearing a bra under her T-shirt.

"What do you mean?" she gasped when I lightly squeezed her nipple between my thumb and forefinger.

"You lit the candles before the power went out." Reality intruded when another punishing gust of wind blasted the house, rattling the windows. "Is there anything you need to check on?"

"Let me just light the other candles." She shimmied out from between my body and the counter, grabbing the lighter and dashing around. As she lit the candles, light glimmered in the space.

She pushed her bedroom door open, glancing over to me. "This way the heat from the woodstove will carry in there, so I won't freeze tonight."

Crossing over to meet her halfway, I stopped at the end of the couch. "I don't think you'll be cold tonight."

"No?"

I shook my head and waited, giving her a chance to step away and slow down this insanity. She didn't. Instead, she lifted a hand, trailing her fingertips along my stubbled jawline before she leaned up for another mind-melding kiss.

This time, I pulled her into a full body clench as I took deep sips of her, feeding off the fire that burned so hot between us. Her curves were soft against me and my cock nestled right in the cradle of her hips. I savored the feel of it when she rocked against me.

Needing air, again, I lifted my head and turned, catching her hand. She tumbled into my lap when I sat down on the couch and gave her a light tug. Fucking perfect. Her knees fell to the sides of my thighs. Without missing a beat, she threaded a hand in my hair and caught my mouth in another breath-stealing kiss.

My hands got busy, shoving up her T-shirt. Her skin was silky soft, and the fabric of her shirt bunched on my wrists. She reached down, catching the hem and lifting it up and over her head. The sound of it rumpling as it fell to the floor mingled with the other sensations racing through me.

Cammi half-naked in my lap with flickering shadows on her skin was a sight to behold.

"You're so fucking beautiful," I murmured as I pressed open kisses in the valley between her breasts.

I cupped one in my palm, savoring the lush weight as I leaned forward, circling my tongue around her nipple, giving it a suck and lightly grazing my teeth as I drew away. She let out a breathy whimper and shifted restlessly on my lap.

When I lifted my head, she protested, "You have too many clothes on."

I chuckled. "Should we see who can strip the fastest?"

Her hair swung around her shoulders when she shook her head. "We should just get naked."

With that bold comment, she shimmied off my lap and pushed her sweatpants down over her hips. I threw my T-shirt aside, only to open my eyes and discover she was wearing a pair of hot pink silk panties. I wasn't ready for those to go yet.

She had just curled her fingers over the elastic when I caught her hand. "Not yet, sweetheart."

Her dark eyes held mine and she bit the corner of her lip, which sent a hot surge of blood to my groin. She arched a brow, giving me a pointed look. "You lost the race."

"There was a race?" I murmured as I stood and

quickly tugged off my clothes. As I stood there, in nothing more than my thin cotton briefs, I realized that if I had a condom it was in my glove compartment.

As if she read my mind, Cammi dashed away, giving me an absolutely delicious view of her bottom in those pink panties. A moment later, she came out of the bathroom with an entire box of condoms, still sealed.

"That's ambitious," I teased when she set them on the coffee table.

She rolled her eyes. "This place used to be a rental. Those were here when I bought it and since the box wasn't even open..." Her words faded as she pressed her palm on my chest, pushing me back. In another moment, we were right back where we'd been, tumbling into the hazy, lightning-hot need.

Our kisses blurred from one to the next. We took turns gulping in air, while her hands were busy everywhere. She mapped my chest and arms, as I savored her silky skin and the sweet give of her curves.

All the while, need built in me, the pressure spinning tightly. I trailed my fingers on the sensitive skin on the inside of her thighs, pushing that pink silk out of the way and delving into her slick, hot core. She cried out, rocking into my touch. We spun into kiss after kiss, a slow, teasing exploration of touch, all the while she rippled around my fingers.

Within minutes, Cammi was stretched out on the couch. Somewhere along the way she'd ditched her panties, which was now exactly what I wanted. Sliding my palms up her calves, I pushed her thighs apart and licked into her folds, just as I sank two fingers inside.

Her body arched as tremors rippled through her as she let out a sharp cry. She was already at the edge.

Her scent and musky flavor surrounded me as I teased her higher and higher until her channel clamped down on my fingers.

She was still trembling when I finally kicked off my briefs. When I reached for that box of condoms, I had to fumble to tear off the plastic and open it. I made quick work of that and smoothed on a condom in a matter of seconds. By that point, I was near desperation.

I absolutely *had* to bury myself inside of her. I eased my weight over her, but she was impatient, curling her legs around my hips and pulling me to her. I stole another kiss before I drew back and notched my cockhead into her entrance.

Chapter Eighteen

CAMMI

There was a sheen of sweat on my skin. The firelight flickering on Elias illuminated his muscled form. The man was in such good shape, he was sculpture worthy.

My heartbeat was thundering, echoing through my body. I felt the thick crown of his cock at my entrance and craved the fullness. We breathed together. On an exhalation, he filled me in a swift surge. The pleasure was intense, almost intoxicating, as I closed my eyes.

I took a ragged breath, opening my eyes just as Elias said my name. Staring into his piercing gaze, I felt stripped bare, inside and out.

It felt so, *so* good to be with him. He was magic with his hands and his mouth. Yet, I'd convinced myself it was just for fun. Until now. With his muscled chest pressed against me as he rested his weight on his elbows, I could feel his heartbeat pounding in tune with mine as we stared at each other. We held completely still for several beats of my heart.

My body moved of its own accord, rocking restlessly into him. Because he seemed to know precisely what I needed, he gave it to me, drawing back and filling me again. His pace started slow and measured, but then I was gasping and chasing after another sweet release. It felt as if a string was cinching tighter and tighter inside, pressure building to a crescendo.

I was shameless, begging, "Harder, please."

"Whatever you need, sweetheart." He pressed a hard kiss on my neck.

One more deep stroke, and everything drew tight before it snapped loose and sent sparks scattering through my body. My climax was still reverberating when I felt him go taut as he shuddered and let out a raw cry.

He fell against me, and I savored the weight of him. He didn't linger though, shifting immediately and rolling over so he was underneath me. I felt as if I'd been cast ashore after a storm, resting on his muscled frame as I gasped for air.

After a few moments, the sounds of the storm outside punctured my awareness, and I lifted my head. Elias's eyes opened, his thick lashes sweeping up. I brushed my mussed hair away from my face. "That was more than kissing."

He chuckled at my comment, leaning up to press another kiss on the side of my neck. I shivered and realized I could go another round with him. That was something to contemplate.

He rolled his head to the side, checking the fire. "Does your heat run without power?" he asked as he looked back at me.

I nodded. "Yeah, but it's just my back-up propane heater. Between the fire and that, it should keep the house warm. I'm guessing we won't get power anytime soon."

We eventually untangled ourselves. We took a shower together, and it was heaven. Because Elias teased me to another orgasm with his fingers, and I thought maybe he might spoil me.

I fell asleep, wrapped in his strong arms with a distant voice in the corner of my mind wondering just how much trouble I was getting myself into.

———

Elias let out a moan of satisfaction and leaned his elbow on the counter. "You really do make the best coffee in the world."

It was ridiculous, but I flushed at his compliment. "I don't know if my home coffee is as good. I don't have my high-end espresso maker here," I commented, gesturing toward my small espresso machine. It was on the fancy side, but definitely not top-shelf like the one in my coffee truck.

He took another slow swallow of his coffee, and my eyes traced the motion of his throat. Sweet hell. Even that was sexy. I was in trouble, *serious* trouble.

He set his mug down and held my gaze. It felt as if little sparks danced through the air between the line of our eyes.

"It's just as good." Turning on his stool with coffee in hand, he looked out my front windows.

The storm had blown away by morning, and the power had flickered on only a few moments after we came awake this morning. Waking up with Elias spooned behind me was beyond incredible. It felt pure and good. Never mind that he rolled me over and had his way with me. Never mind that I was a needy girl with him and any resistance I tried to talk myself into was swept away after nothing more than one hot kiss from him.

Then, we showered again. For me, I needed a

morning shower no matter what. It was just how I
woke up. Of course, seeing soap bubbles rolling over
his muscled back and chest, well, everywhere, only left
me toeing the edge of desire all over again. Afterwards, I made pancakes and coffee.

"Last night was a windy storm," he commented as
he scanned the view.

My house was situated far back on a bluff that
looked out over the harbor and into the bay. Several
tree limbs had fallen in my yard, and a whimsical drag-
onfly flag I'd mounted on the corner of my deck had
blown loose and fallen into a rumple in the yard.

"I'm grateful only my windshield took a hit," I
replied.

Elias turned in his chair stool to face me again. "I'll
drive you over there. Maybe call your insurance
company this morning?"

I experienced a stab of grief. This would be a situation when I would usually call my parents. But the last
two years had been two swift losses. First, my father
died in his sleep from a heart attack. Then, my mother
followed with complications from diabetes only a year
later. I missed them, and there was nothing to do
about it.

I mentally cast about, thinking of any friends that
I could call. All of my friends would gladly help, but
most of them were probably dealing with children and
other busy-ness this morning.

"I won't be driving it until I get the windshield
fixed. Hopefully nothing else is wrong inside. Thank
you again for thinking to put the tarp over it."

"Let's hope it held through the night," he said.

"I'll call the insurance company and maybe they
can arrange for somebody to fix it today."

He nodded. "I'll drop you off, and if you need a

ride this afternoon, just text me." I opened my mouth to protest, but he added, "I'm not headed out to the resort today. I've got several flights scheduled, so I'll be freed up late this afternoon."

"Okay," I chirped, feeling uncertain and not wanting to rely on him, but realizing no matter what I'd be inconveniencing somebody.

Elias dropped me off at work, giving me a lingering kiss. He left me hot and bothered in my coffee truck and wondering just what I was getting myself into. I'd already called my insurance company, and they'd made arrangements for someone to assess my windshield and see if it could be replaced here, or have to be taken into a shop.

Later that afternoon, I was busy and relieved because my windshield was brand new, and I didn't need to rely on anyone for a ride. I was still wondering in the back of my mind, in that silly, foolish, ever-hopeful corner, if Elias would come by for coffee.

You're just wondering because he would anyway. All very true, but that was total bullshit.

"Hey, Cammi," a voice said.

I glanced up to see Marley Hamilton standing there with her husband and their daughter. They were in line behind the couple Amy was just ringing up.

"Hey, how's it going?" I replied.

"Well, the storm last night was no fun," Marley commented.

The sun was bright and the sky was clear today, although there was still a salty breeze coming off the harbor. Marley's auburn hair was pulled back in a ponytail, which twirled in the air with a gust of wind as she smiled back at me.

Gage added, "Yeah, we had a tree fall on one end of the ski lodge. Only minor damage, but that's why we're in town today. We're picking up some things from the hardware store."

Their daughter, Holly, chirped, "Lumber."

I smiled at Holly as they stepped to the front of the line. I was already prepping the coffees for the family in front of them and handed them over as I continued to talk, "I know. A limb fell on my windshield here. Thank goodness it just shattered it. It's already fixed."

"I'm glad that's all that happened." Marley paused, glancing around as several more cars pulled into the parking area. "You're busy early this year," she observed while Gage ordered for them.

"I know. It seems like every year things pick up a little earlier. How are things out at the lodge?"

"Well, the skiers are slowing down, but the restaurant's always busy. We usually have a little lull right now because the skiing isn't great and the trails aren't good for hiking yet. In another month or two, the lodge will be full of guests again."

Just then, my eyes lifted. I didn't know how, but somehow I knew Elias was here. I was instantly flustered and tore my gaze away from his truck—his freaking truck sped my pulse—and tried to focus on Marley.

"Rumor has it you're looking into buying Misty Mountain."

"Where did you hear that?" I squeaked.

"From Hannah. I think you should do it. I love it there, but you do have better coffee."

"I'm seriously looking into it. If I can make it work, I will," I replied just as Amy told me their order, and Elias approached the back of the line.

His eyes met mine, and the look there singed me. Gage returned as he adjusted Holly in his arms. She was just past three years old and a wiggly toddler these days.

"Good to see you, man," he said, addressing Elias with a quick smile.

Gage was incredibly handsome with brown hair and smoky grey eyes. Yet, I felt nothing when I stared at him. It was only Elias who could slay me with a mere glance.

"Doing well," Elias said with a nod. "Back in the air, and that's all that matters."

Gage chuckled. "I get it. I'm not so great at being laid up myself."

Elias nodded, just as Holly took that moment to burst into tears when she reached for her mother's coffee and Marley pulled it out of reach.

Gage comforted her, and she calmed down a little before narrowing her eyes at her mother. Marley caught my eyes. "She wants anything I have these days."

I happened to look in Elias's direction at that moment, and he was eyeing Holly with what I could only describe as skepticism.

Gage caught the same look. "It's worth it, man."

Elias grinned and gave something of a non-committal reply that I didn't quite catch. After they left, another group of customers rolled in. I didn't get a chance to talk to Elias, although he did pause to comment, "I see your windshield's all taken care of. I'll text you about this weekend."

He left, and I wondered. I was picking apart his interaction with Gage and Marley, wondering if he wanted kids or not.

Why are you wondering about kids already? This is what got you in trouble before with Joel. You need to pump the brakes.

So very true. I got way ahead of myself with Joel. I wanted so badly to find someone to be serious with that I was positive I'd missed some major red flags that might've clued me into the fact I'd stumbled into a lying asshat. While I wasn't worried about Elias being an asshat, I was worried about jumping in too deeply. Unfortunately, I was pretty sure I was already in over my head.

Chapter Nineteen

ELIAS

"Looking good," Nora said at my shoulder, her tone teasing. I glanced sideways.

"What do you mean?"

If I'd wondered if she was giving me a little hell, I knew for sure with the sly gleam in her eyes. "You're totally rocking that suit. And Cammi looks great with you. You're treating her like a real date."

I shifted my shoulders in said suit jacket. "She *is* a real date."

We were at the fundraiser Daphne had planned and cajoled all of us into attending. Based on the crowd alone, it was a smashing success. We were giving away some pricey flights for tourists. Everyone who wasn't a business person donating something had paid a hefty fee for dinner. With Daphne in charge of the food, it was worth every penny.

"Daphne outdid herself with the food," I commented to Nora. "Also, you look great yourself."

My compliment was entirely platonic, but she did look great. Nora's dark hair fell down her back, straight and glossy. She usually wore it in a braid, or ponytail, or a messy bun. Her big brown eyes were set off with a hint of smoky shadow. She wore a pretty dress, and I doubted any of us missed the way Gabriel could hardly keep his eyes off of her.

Case in point: as I glanced around, I saw him standing a few feet away, talking with Grant and Flynn. Every few seconds, his eyes darted to Nora. He looked like he was a combination of angry and turned on.

"You're giving Gabriel fits, by the way," I added.

Nora's eyes narrowed to daggers. "I don't know what you're talking about."

"Okay," I said easily. It was no sweat off my back if they wanted to keep denying the sparking chemistry between them.

I felt before I saw Cammi returning to my side. She had departed for a restroom break. Turning, that now familiar jolt of electricity sizzled down my spine when I saw her. She looked stunning tonight. Her hair swung in a clean line right along her shoulders as she turned and smiled at someone who said her name. When she reached me, my breath seized in my lungs for a moment. She didn't need makeup, but fuck me, she'd added smoky eyeshadow and a dash of lip gloss, and all I could think was I needed to kiss it off. The blue in her eyes was even brighter, if possible.

She'd worn a navy silk dress that hugged her curves like a lover. I was jealous of the fabric itself, an entirely new experience for me. I was torn between wanting to run my hands over that silk, or tearing it off of her. The only thing holding me back was I did have *some* manners.

When she stopped beside me, I didn't even try to play it cool and let my palm slide down her back, savoring the warmth of her skin in the V opening before it crossed over the silk and came to rest just above her bottom. I had to forcibly check myself to keep from giving her sweet bottom a squeeze.

"Need more champagne?" I asked as I saw a waiter weaving through the crowd with a tray of champagne flutes.

"In a minute," she said. "I'm sure one of the waiters will pass by us soon. Daphne's done a great job."

"She always does," Nora chimed in.

Cammi smiled. "She has. It's nice you all have her out at the resort."

"Tell me about it," I replied. "We're all grateful she and Flynn are together. Otherwise, I'm sure she could find better places to be a chef."

"We *are* lucky," Nora chimed in. "She seems to genuinely love it though. I don't know if she would leave. There's something to be said for just being where you want to be."

I knew that deeply. Because I was where I wanted to be in Alaska. Cammi was starting to make me wonder if maybe this didn't need just to be a place to find peace. Maybe I could have a little bit more than that. That was unsettling. Because letting anyone matter too much was hard for me and something I'd fought against.

The fundraiser moved along, and I was relieved to have Cammi with me. She was fun and easy and knew everyone I did and then some. About halfway through the night, we were sitting at a table with Flynn, Daphne, Diego, Nora, and Tucker. My arm was resting across her shoulders because I didn't care that all my friends knew I wanted her.

Cammi nearly jumped in her seat, her shoulder stiffening under my arm. When I glanced down, she had a look of horror on her face. No one else had noticed yet because they were busy talking, so I leaned over, speaking low in her ear. "Everything okay?"

"Uh, well, that guy? The one I didn't know was married?" At my nod, she continued, "He's here with another woman. I don't care about it for me, but oh my God. He's probably doing the same thing all over again."

I followed her line of sight, my eyes landing on the man I'd seen her encounter at the lodge restaurant. Sure enough, the woman he was with was definitely *not* the woman I'd seen him with that night. They also appeared *very* together. He had his arm around her, and she was laughing at something he said.

"So, he's a total asshole, but then you knew that."

Cammi let out a huff of breath. "God. I'm such an idiot."

I caught her chin in my hand, turning her to look at me. "Don't blame yourself. He lied, plain and simple. And, don't change who you are either. Trust me, it's no good going through life doubting people. Would you blame her if you knew he'd lied to her about who he was too?"

Two bright red spots appeared on her cheeks and her eyes looked anguished as she shook her head. "No, but—"

I shook my head quickly. "No buts. He lied, and you believed him. That's it."

Cammi's swallow was audible as she nodded slowly. The color in her cheeks faded, and she gave me a small smile. "Thank you. I'm totally over him, but it just makes me sick."

"Should I go punch him for you?" I was dead serious. I wouldn't ruin Daphne's fundraiser, but I'd take him outside.

Her eyes widened. "No! You're not serious, are you?"

"Completely. You didn't deserve his lies, and neither does the woman he's with. Even though I don't know her, I'm not a fan of liars."

My own history in this regard was twisted with bitterness. Hell, cheating and the betrayal of my friend clung to me. I missed him too. That was the fucked up thing about betrayal. These were the reasons why I'd never intended to get serious again. There was one catch. I hadn't thought I was capable of feeling enough for someone again.

Cammi was blowing my perceptions about my ability to control my emotions to smithereens.

"No, don't do that," she said, slowly shaking her head. "I'm horrified, but it's strangely a relief to see he's still up to his old tricks. It wasn't just me."

"Maybe you should let his wife know."

She chewed on her bottom lip, distracting me instantly. This time, I didn't hold back, leaning down and catching her lips in a kiss. I dove into her sweet mouth. She didn't hesitate when I swept in, just for a second, and her sassy tongue glided against mine.

When I drew back, she let out a wondering laugh. "You do make me forget everything, including where we are."

I heard Diego's chuckle from across the table and cast him a quick look, giving an unrepentant shrug.

"Told you it was a real date," Nora called from where she sat between Diego and Tucker.

"We all knew that," Daphne said. "Now leave them alone."

Daphne might be petite, but she was fierce, and we all generally did whatever she said.

What happened with Cammi should have given me

pause. And yet, it was so obvious she'd unknowingly walked into an affair. I hated that my friend's death and betrayal were tangled up, but I knew her actions weren't like his. He'd known exactly what he was doing when he screwed around with my then-girlfriend.

Much as I wanted to go out of my way and rough up the man who betrayed Cammi, I didn't. I didn't know what to think about how I'd tapped into a vein of protectiveness I didn't even know I had.

I remembered Greg dying. I remembered my ex sobbing uncontrollably over the phone, at which point I realized she'd been having an affair with my best friend. I remembered her trying to fix it, but that was it for me. I remembered my physical pain and tumbling into the oblivion of opiates. Those pharmaceutical companies spun a poison type of a scab. Between my physical and emotional pain, it had all been too tempting to lose myself in numbness.

I was thinking about that later when I saw that man look over at Cammi and his eyes lingered for a moment. My hand was resting on her back and I slid it around to curl over her hip possessively. Because she was mine. Even if I wasn't quite ready to plumb the depths of what *mine* meant.

I rode the edge of a fierce need all night. By the time Daphne announced the winners of various high-end giveaways, I just needed to get out of there. Because I needed Cammi.

Chapter Twenty

CAMMI

It was late, and the stars glittered in the darkness. We drove along the highway with the moonlight shimmering on the ocean's surface to one side. My body felt fizzy, bubbly with desire and this uncertain emotion centered on Elias. I couldn't say what I'd expected tonight, but I definitely had *not* expected him to be so public with me.

Mind you, I didn't mind the PDA, not one bit. I'd been startled to see Joel there, and his presence could've ruined my night, but it hadn't. While I was well over him, his appearance at my coffee truck and attempt to talk to me had thrown me. I was relieved he'd seen me with Elias because hopefully he knew to leave me alone from now on. It felt deliciously good to be beside Elias with his arm around my waist, holding me almost possessively.

Seeing Joel in the presence of Elias was a neon reminder of everything Joel wasn't. Elias was like the authentic version of the faded image Joel tried to project. Without any effort, Elias exuded raw, almost primitive masculinity. And, oh-my-heart and every cell in my body was the man handsome. My parts were still quivering just from being with him all night.

His energy was intense with an almost pensive quality to it that I wasn't sure how to interpret as he drove toward home. He reached across the bench seat in his truck—which, by the way, was freaking awesome—and caught my hand and gave it a little tug.

"Come here," he murmured, his voice low and gravelly.

I didn't need to be told twice. I unbuckled my seatbelt and slid into the center.

"Buckle up, sweetheart," he added.

I did, because we were going over sixty miles per hour on the highway heading back to Diamond Creek.

"Thanks for coming tonight." He slid his palm, strong and sure, over my thigh.

"Thanks for inviting me. The food was amazing and the party was nice. We don't have many events like that."

"Daphne will be thrilled. Remind me how long the drive is back to Diamond Creek."

We'd driven north to Kenai where the event was hosted. "Just under two hours," I offered.

He made a sound in his throat. I kind of thought it was a growl, but that seemed a little weird. Until he hooked his fingers over the hem of my silky dress and slid the fabric up my thigh. Although it was cool out tonight, I'd known it would be warm inside the crowded event, so I wasn't even wearing stockings. The feel of his calloused palm on the inside of my thigh had me shivering all over. I was wet, because I'd been wet all night. Elias had that effect on me.

"I can't wait that long."

Elias's voice sent a quiver through me. "Wait that long for what?"

"You."

His palm slid up further, cupping my mound, his fingers teasing over the damp silk. I couldn't help the ragged breath that escaped when my pussy clenched. Elias sped up slightly before turning abruptly into a drive that I knew led to a clearing. It might've been dark, and I might've been half out of my mind with lust, but I knew this road. I could see the map of it in my mind. In the summer, there were picnic tables where people stopped for lunch on pretty days.

The narrow road passed through a cluster of trees and opened up to a small viewing area. Elias turned into a parking spot, and the truck came to a jerky stop. I was sure we were parked outside the lines, but it was deserted, and I didn't care.

He slid the bench seat back and pulled me into his lap. Kissing him was simply the best. He was kind of bossy about it, but then so was I. He chuckled when I nipped lightly at his bottom lip. Our hands were everywhere, and my dress was in a rumple around my hips. I shimmied off his lap to gain access.

I had his slacks unbuttoned and his zipper down in no time, letting out a happy sigh when I curled my palm over his velvety hot length. His head fell back against the seat as I stroked and rubbed my thumb over the cum beading at the top.

I needed to taste him and leaned over to lick that drop away, a wave of satisfaction rolling through me when he let out a ragged groan as I took him into my mouth. His taste was musky and salty, dancing across my tongue. I teased him for a few moments, sucking deeply and stroking with my fist before his hand tangled in my hair.

"I need to be inside you," he said bluntly.

I straightened, artlessly shoving my panties down,

laughing when they got caught on one ankle. He produced a condom out of his wallet and was smoothing it on as I rose up over him.

"Come here, sweetheart," he murmured.

I needed no orders, but I absolutely loved when he gave them. In a moment, he was guiding himself into my entrance. I tried to go slow, but I couldn't help it. I felt half drunk on pleasure as he seated himself deeply inside me. I let out a low hum, my hips rocking instantly.

Elias had one hand curled around my bare hip just under where my dress was rumpled, and the other slid up my back as he levered me forward slightly and caught my lips in a fierce kiss.

When he drew back, my eyes opened, and his were there waiting, hot and intent. My heart gave a hard kick. Then, he was notching into me and filling me again, and we rocked together as I chased my sweet release. I had no sense of time, I was made of sensation and pleasure. The slick fusion of our joining created just enough pressure on my clit that my release was racing upon me. I came in a noisy rush, just as he followed me over the edge. His fingers dug into my skin, and I needed the touch, the pressure to anchor me in the storm of this moment.

Afterward, I was a boneless heap in his lap. He held me in his relaxed hold, and I thought I was just the easiest girl ever when it came to him. I didn't even know what to do about it. I felt as if I'd been caught in a riptide. This man, who had been distant with me for so long, turned me into a puddle. I didn't even know what to do with myself, yet I savored being held by him, cocooned in his strength and protectiveness.

Eventually, we untangled ourselves and put our clothes to rights.

Chapter Twenty-One

ELIAS

It wasn't enough to lose myself in the rush of need for Cammi with such fierceness that I had to pull off on the side of the highway and take her in my truck like a teenage boy who didn't have anywhere private to go. Even after that, I needed her right beside me with her fingers laced through mine where my hand rested on her thigh for the rest of the drive home.

Once again, I texted Flynn and told him I'd meet him at the plane hangar in the morning because I sure as hell wasn't driving home to sleep without Cammi.

———

Another evening

"Don't even," Gabriel said, narrowing his eyes at Flynn across the table.

Flynn's lips kicked up at one corner. "Don't even, what?"

"Win this fucking game," Gabriel muttered. "I haven't gotten a good hand yet tonight."

We were in the kitchen at the resort, playing cards. Tonight, the game of choice was rummy. We'd fallen into this pattern of getting together late once or twice a week after the guests were all in their rooms.

Diego arced his gaze around the table before laying a winning hand down.

Flynn chuckled. "Here's what I had. Not likely to win. But you know what they say."

"I know what you're gonna tell me," Gabriel interjected. "It's not the hand you're dealt, but how you play it."

"You're too impatient," I offered.

"You don't win that often," Gabriel countered.

"True, probably because I don't really care." I set my cards down and drained my bottle of beer. Looking to Flynn, I added, "I'm really liking our new relationship with Diamond Creek Brewery."

"Aren't we all?" Diego offered from across the table.

Flynn cocked his head to the side as he gathered the cards and began shuffling. "That's all Daphne's doing. I never had time to nurture those business connections. Plus, we get a discount because once a month she helps them with their menu planning for free."

"I think she loves doing that stuff," Diego chimed in.

"Oh, hell yeah, she does," Flynn agreed. "I swear, it's a good thing she loves me the way I am. I'm sure she'd prefer a guy who would seduce her with food conversation. Man, she can talk food for hours."

We all laughed. "I don't think you need to worry on that account," I offered.

Flynn's gaze sobered as he dealt the cards. "No, I don't think I do, which still blows my mind almost every day."

Diego caught my eyes. "You're on your way, man."

"On my way to what?" I gathered up my cards, quickly sorting them.

"To being as whipped as Flynn," Tucker offered with a roll of his eyes.

My heart twisted in my chest the moment I thought of Cammi. I knew my friends might be right, but I wasn't ready to have a group chat about it. I shrugged lightly instead. "Maybe, maybe not." When I lifted my eyes again, I remembered why having old friends was challenging occasionally. Every guy at this table knew what happened in the last relationship I'd let go anywhere. The friend who'd ruined it wasn't here with us—Greg.

We'd all been tight in the Air Force. We had other friends we kept in touch with but this crew here was like family. There's a reason we all ended up landing here with Flynn. Greg probably would've landed here too. Except maybe not because I probably would've found out he was fucking my girlfriend on the side, the very girlfriend I'd contemplated asking to marry me. I hadn't taken that step, but it was out there. And, lo and behold, she was screwing around with one of my best friends on the side. That kind of betrayal stings and cuts both ways—*deep*. Even worse, Greg had screwed over another one of our friends too.

I never said it out loud, but after that, I figured I wasn't going to ever trust anybody enough like that. That was the crazy thing about Cammi, I trusted her completely.

Diego held my eyes for a few beats, but he said nothing further. My friends, because they were that fucking solid, didn't speak aloud the ghost that dashed through our conversation.

We played for a while more and then Flynn went to bed because Daphne was there waiting. Tucker and Gabriel decided to head into town, while Diego and I walked back to the staff house.

We were standing in the kitchen, and I was draining a glass of water when Diego asked, "You let that shit go yet?"

I knew what he meant, but because I could be a stubborn fool, I asked, "What shit?"

"Greg and Sandra."

I set the water glass down and crossed over to flop onto the couch. Although four guys lived here, we kept it pretty clean. Diego was a bit of a mother hen, always tidying things up. He was also a damn good cook and would cook for us here if we missed dinner over at the resort. He followed me, sitting down at an angle across from me on the giant sectional couch, which was seriously comfortable, by the way.

Because he was a good guy and the best kind of friend, he turned on the news. I knew he wasn't going to drop the topic, but he would give me the gift of some background noise.

"I think so," I finally said. "It burns. Greg was my friend. If he'd survived, I could've given him hell and then moved on. We probably wouldn't have stayed close, but I just fucking hate how it all played out. He's dead, and I still fucking miss him sometimes. But he fucked me over behind my back with my girl. I'm actually more upset with him than her, or I was. With her, I let that go. It is what it is. Cheating is the oldest betrayal in the book."

Diego had switched the channel to some singing

reality show. I was temporarily distracted. "Dude, that singer definitely won't be winning."

"Agreed. Yeah, cheating happens to plenty of people. But, it's not always with a good friend. I just wanna know if you're going to give Cammi a real shot."

I silently groaned. Diego was *that* friend, the one I usually turned to when I needed a good sounding board. The flip side to that was he had opinions, fucking opinions, about emotional shit. He was seriously tight with his family. When he fell, because it was a foregone conclusion he would fall, I sure hoped that girl was ready because this man was fierce.

"I'm gonna try. Is that good enough for you?"

He chuckled. "I think you already have. I just don't want you to let your baggage get in the way."

"Anybody ever tell you that you took the wrong career path?"

"What should I be doing?" he countered.

"You should've been a therapist. You're always all up in my business, and not just mine."

He threw his head back with a laugh. "I think I'd be too blunt for that. It's only people I love I give a little hell to when it's necessary."

"I am forever grateful you're my friend, man." I meant it even if he drove me crazy on occasion.

He thumped his fist over his heart. "Same. I know you got my back."

"Speaking of falling for someone, you know it's going to be rough when you do. Because your turn will come, it's only a matter of time."

Diego's gaze sobered. "I know. I've been in love before, so I know how hard it can bite."

I wanted to press, but I was honestly tired. "I know damn straight this guy ain't winning," I said, shifting away from that heavy topic to the next singer on the show.

"Sure thing. Wanna bet five bucks?"

"Deal. I vote on whoever follows this guy."

"You're not even gonna wait to listen?" Diego countered.

"Nope. Speaking of five bucks, Faith told me you owe her," I said, suddenly remembering my call with her.

Diego chuckled. "Oh, right. She called looking for you, and we bet on the game. I'll give you extra if you win this bet."

Turned out I actually won that five dollars, and Diego gave me the five more he owed Faith. Of course, I bought Diego's coffee the next morning when Cammi refused to charge me for mine, so I didn't keep it for long.

I paid for mine with a kiss and left her blushing as Diego chuckled, and we headed out for another delivery flight.

Chapter Twenty-Two

CAMMI

"Well, underwriting approved it," Shirley-at-the-bank, as I mentally called her in my head, said.

"They did?" I squeaked.

Susie, who sat beside me across from Shirley, lifted her fists in triumph. "Yes! I knew you were in a good position to do this, and I was right."

Shirley laughed softly as she looked between us. "She was right. Now, go celebrate."

"That's it?" I asked as I looked between them.

"For now. The closing is scheduled for next Friday," Shirley added.

I almost started crying, but I didn't want to cry in front of Shirley, so I managed to keep it together. I burst into tears when Susie hugged me in the parking lot a few minutes later.

"Let's go celebrate with lunch there. The sellers are ecstatic. They wanted somebody local. You're your own competition now, girl."

I stepped back, and Susie produced a small package of tissues from her purse. I took several out and dabbed at my eyes before blowing my nose. Her brown eyes twinkled with her smile as she waited.

"Now, I've got to figure out what I'm gonna do with a whole café. I can't believe it."

Susie was on the bossy side as friends went, and she bundled me into her car and had me over at Misty Mountain Café inside of a few minutes. The owners weren't there, but the staff knew I was buying the café and everyone was excited. We snagged a table in the corner, and I ordered my favorite sandwich there, the pesto turkey with gouda cheese.

"I think I'll stick with their menu at first until I figure everything out. I'm kind of freaking out," I said as I looked over at Susie.

She tucked her brown curls behind her ears and nodded. "It'll be all right. I do their accounting so that's all set. Don't forget we budgeted that as part of your business plan. The accounting here is more complicated than what you've got at your little truck. For now, enjoy your lunch and just breathe. Also, catch me up on Elias."

My cheeks got hot before I could formulate a reply. Susie burst out laughing. "I knew it!"

"Knew what?"

"That maybe there was a thing with you two."

I took a breath, willing my blush to fade and knowing it wouldn't. "Okay, fine, there's a thing."

Our sandwiches arrived, and we paused to start eating. Susie only let me have a few bites before she circled her hand in the air.

"Okay, okay. I don't know what to do about him."

"How about you fill me in? What's the status? I know you went to the fundraiser together up in Kenai, but, what else?"

"I'm not gonna give you all the details, but let's just say he's great with his hands."

Susie's eyes took on a gleam. "Of course he is. He's got great hands and a hot bod to go with them."

Her eyes sobered. She must have picked up on the worry spinning inside me. I'd never been great at keeping a straight face. "What is it?" she pressed.

I almost burst into tears and had to take a bite of my sandwich to chew my feelings under control. Bless Susie's heart, but she let me do that. Much as she could be a pushy, nosy friend, she cared deeply.

After a few bites, I began, "I don't know. You know I've never been good at the casual thing. Which was why it was such a disaster when Joel lied to me, and it ended up being a fucking affair. I really like Elias, and I don't know what he thinks, or how to handle it."

"Well, we know Elias isn't lying to you about who he is. We all know who he is. He's worked for Flynn for what, five years now?"

"Something like that." Now came the hard part— being honest with my friend about just how left behind I felt in life. "It's hard. Because I want to find someone. I want to have kids before it's too late. I just don't know if I can trust anyone enough, or myself for that matter. I mean, why would anybody trust me after what happened?"

Susie looked crushed. "Sweetie." She reached for one of my hands, curling hers over it and squeezing it tightly. "That wasn't your fault. You didn't know Joel was married. He didn't even give you his real name. And, you're only thirty-two. You have plenty of time to have kids."

My eyes were stinging again, and she was squeezing my hand a little too hard. She was kind of fierce like that. I managed a shaky smile and knuckled at my tears with my free hand. "You're kind of hurting my hand," I said.

Her eyebrows flew up. "Oh! Sorry." She eased her grip and released my hand.

"I know what you're saying is true, but it just feels all so impossible. I like Elias, and I know he's not lying about who he is, but I don't know if he wants what I want. Maybe he doesn't want kids. I *really* want kids. It's kind of a deal breaker for me."

Susie paused to take a bite of her sandwich, and that let me know all I needed to know. She actually had to think about her answer. Her opinions were usually flying out like horses at the start of a race.

We ate in silence for a few moments before she replied, "Look, obviously I have no idea if Elias wants kids. But all you can do is try. And it's better that you know what you want now, than to stumble ahead and find out it's not a good fit. Plus, catch me on a bad day and I don't want kids. I'll give one of mine away when they're in the middle of a tantrum. No problem." She waved her hand in the air and rolled her eyes.

I couldn't help but laugh at that. "True. Ugh. Romance is a pain in the ass."

"I guess it's not great to have most of your friends married with kids now, huh?" she pressed gently. Gentle wasn't really her approach, which again made me feel obnoxiously fragile.

"I'm really happy for all of you. Seriously. But, yeah, I often feel a little behind the times."

"I want you to do me a favor," Susie said.

"Sure," I replied, not thinking much of it. If my friend asked for a favor, I'd be glad to do it.

"Talk to Elias about this."

My eyes flew wide open, and I almost choked on the last bite of my sandwich. After washing it down with some water, I asked, "Are you insane? I think it's a little too soon to have the kids conversation."

"Really? Why let things go further? If you know he doesn't want to have kids, find out now. You also need to get over that crazy thing in your head that people are going to think you're a bad person for stumbling into a situation where you didn't know what was going on. Talk to him about that too."

"I already did."

"Oh. Well, good for you. You've got this."

That was Susie, my personal cheerleader.

————

I went to the coffee truck after our lunch and dove into a busy afternoon. Working was a relief. I had a lot to think about between getting the loan approved for the purchase of Misty Mountain Café and Susie's thoughts on Elias.

Immediately after a rush of mid-afternoon customers coming in from the harbor, I looked up to see Fran, Joel's wife. Fuck my life. I was the only one there because Amy had a doctor's appointment this afternoon. She was only gone for an hour, but it was just my bad luck for Joel's wife to show up now.

The only good thing was no one was in line behind her. I managed something resembling a smile. "Hi. Can I help you?" I was relieved I'd said those words so many times that they just came out automatically without any thought necessary. I felt sick to my stomach, and I tried to take a shaky breath.

Fran was quiet for a moment, and then I noticed how tightly her hand was curled around the handle to her purse. I didn't want her to be nervous because she had nothing to fear from me, but it gave me a sliver of hope that maybe she wasn't here to give me hell.

"I came to apologize," she finally said, her words stiff.

"You don't need to apologize to me. I'm the one who should apologize to you. I didn't know Joel was married. I was horrified when I found out, and I still am," I said earnestly.

She nodded slowly and swallowed. "I know now that he was lying to me when he said you knew he was married. I'm the one who slashed your tire that night. I was just feeling a little crazy."

"Um, it's okay. I can imagine the situation felt awful." I paused, contemplating whether to let her know I'd seen Joel at that fundraiser with another woman. I finally decided to just tell her. We might as well be there for each other in some fashion. "Look, this is weird, but I think you should know I saw him with another woman at a fundraiser recently. I don't expect you to trust me, and I'm not telling you to be hurtful. I just think you deserve to know the truth."

Her lips twisted in a bitter smile. "I know. Well, I don't know specifically that you saw them, but I know he's having another affair. I called him on everything when I found out from a mutual friend of ours that he lied to you about everything, including his name. He's an asshole."

My heart ached for this woman. I was over Joel, but the situation still burned because I didn't know how to trust myself anymore. Or, anyone else for that matter. I could only imagine what it felt like for her, considering they were actually married and she had children with him.

"I am *so* sorry," I said fervently. "That sucks. I can't even imagine how you feel."

Her shoulders rose and fell when she took in a deep breath and let it out in a gust. "I'm actually better than I was before the first time. You weren't his first affair, but it was the first time I found out. I felt so inadequate. I was so angry at that point, and I targeted some of it at you. It's all so messed up because we have kids. No matter what happens to my marriage, I have to deal with him because of them. When I found out this time, I was just like, okay, we're done, and it was kind of a relief. I think I knew that at first, but I didn't know how to get to that place. If that makes any sense."

"It does. I don't know what I could do to help, but if there's anything I can do, just let me know."

Fran actually smiled a little at that. "That's sweet of you. You seem like a really nice person. I'm actually divorcing him and moving back to where my parents are in Washington state. I think a fresh start for the kids and me is best. Plus, I'm going to get his business here in the divorce. That was his whole cover for going out of town and making up bullshit about who he was."

"Good for you," I said firmly. "Would you like a coffee? I promise it's good."

"Actually, I would. You're so busy that I doubt you remember me, but I've been here before and this is my favorite coffee shop in Diamond Creek."

"Really? That's awesome. Today's coffee is on the house. Tell me what you want."

Fran got her coffee, and we actually chatted for a little longer. Then, my next wave of people showed up off the boats, and she left. Although she couldn't repair the situation for me, I felt an immense sense of relief for that conversation.

As the afternoon wound down, my phone buzzed

with a text after Amy returned from her doctor's appointment.

Susie: *We're going to yoga class with Tess to celebrate your new business.*

I was up for yoga class, but it seemed like a strange choice for celebration.

Me: *Yoga class?*

Susie: *Yes. There's that new yoga studio. Tess says it's amazing and relaxing. Let's do that, and then, pizza and beer at DC Brewery.*

Me: *Yoga, pizza, and beer. Sounds like a plan.*

I was laughing as I hit send.

Chapter Twenty-Three

ELIAS

I angled the plane in the sky, looking ahead to Diamond Creek. The small town was just coming into view from across the bay. The harbor was visible with boats streaming in slowly from a day of fishing. The roads curved up along the hillside, winding up into the mountains.

A light gust of wind buffeted the plane, and I adjusted to level the plane out after the turn. It felt so good to be flying again. I wiggled my ankle slightly, relieved to feel some flexion. The surgeon had told me I would always have a little trouble with rotation, but all in all, my ankle was back to working order. I was beyond relieved it was my left ankle rather than my right.

As I lowered the plane, I spied a sea lion swimming just outside the harbor entrance and gestured to the passengers to look down as we lowered. Sea lions were massive creatures and easily visible from the air in the shallow waters once you were low enough. I grinned at the oohs and ahhs coming from over my shoulder. As if to show off, an eagle took flight from one of the signs just as we came in for a landing at the airport, giving the passengers a close look as it flew level with us when we came down over the runway.

Alaska's surfeit of wildlife could be so flashy. After we landed and the passengers disembarked, I rolled the plane into the hangar to put it up for the night. As I was doing the evening checks, Flynn came in from the side door, calling over, "How'd it go?"

"Good. Easy flight, happy customers. Best we can ask for."

"Absolutely." He stopped beside me as I hitched my backpack over my shoulder. "Want to go to yoga class with me?"

"I'm sorry, did you say yoga class?"

Flynn looked a little sheepish. "Daphne wants me to go with her."

Diego had just come in and burst out laughing. "Daphne wants you to go to yoga class?"

"Oh, for fuck's sake, guys. Just go with me. We can have dinner at the brewery afterwards."

"Yeah, because yoga followed by beer totally makes sense," I said dryly.

By this point, Diego reached us. He glanced between us. "I'm game."

"What do we need to wear?" I muttered, knowing I was already doomed to be persuaded to join this madness.

Diego chuckled. Meanwhile, Flynn, revealing he'd planned this all along, said, "I had Cat get T-shirts and shorts for you guys out of the laundry."

Diego met my gaze, his lips twitching. "We have no choice. You know that, right?"

"I'll go," I replied with a belabored sigh. I didn't mean it, but it was fun to give Flynn a little grief.

"I'd like to point out that there is no way in fucking hell you would've ever gone to a yoga class before you met Daphne," Diego offered.

Flynn gave us another sheepish smile. "I know. She likes the teacher, and she promised me there were other guys there."

"But why do we have to go with you?" I asked as the three of us turned to leave together. Without needing to discuss it, we each went through the quick motions to close down the office and lock up the plane hangar before walking out to the parking lot.

"Because I need support," Flynn said flatly.

———

"As you lift your arms, take a deep breath in," the yoga teacher said in her soothing voice. "Take a breath all the way into your belly. Let it out, and then slowly lean forward. You can bend your knees as your head comes down if the backs of your thighs feel too tight."

The yoga teacher, Gemma, did seem nice. She was pretty with amber curls that fell to her shoulders and stunning brown eyes. Diego was having trouble keeping his eyes off of her. Meanwhile, Cammi was here too, drawing my eyes to her again and again. I was only half paying attention to the class. She was here with Susie and another friend of hers, Tess.

We got here a little late, and Flynn cast an apologetic look toward Daphne as we hurried to the back of the almost full class.

We did a few balancing postures, and I found my left ankle challenged with that. Despite the distraction of Cammi, I actually liked the class, which surprised me. Afterward, Daphne was talking with Cammi in the parking lot about menu options for her apparently newly acquired café. That gave me an easy excuse to stop and chat with the rest of the group.

"We're grabbing dinner together, do you all wanna come with us?" Susie asked.

"We were already planning on dinner," Daphne said. "It was the only way I could persuade Flynn and the guys to come to yoga. Did you like it?" She looked from Flynn to Diego and then to me. All three of us nodded obediently. Daphne's hazel eyes narrowed. "Are you just humoring me?"

"No, babe," Flynn said as he slid his arm around her waist and dipped his head to dust a kiss on her cheek. "I actually liked it."

"I swear, I did too," I offered. "I didn't realize how tight my back was though." I absently rubbed my hand over my lower back. "I hope I don't end up sore from all that stretching."

Gemma happened to come out at that moment, hearing my comment. She smiled over at us as she locked the door. "You might be at first. Feel free to come back. The first four classes are free, so I promise I'm not trying to make money off of you."

She stopped beside us, and I didn't miss Diego's gaze sweeping over her. He was enough of a gentleman not to ogle her. When her eyes landed on his, I was pretty sure there was a little sizzle in the air. Of course, perhaps I was confusing the sizzle with the fact that whenever I was near Cammi, my body felt like an engine revving.

"Thank you all for coming," she added.

Tess smiled widely. "I told you I would get more students coming to your classes."

"We'll come back," Susie chimed in.

"I'll definitely be back," Daphne offered.

"How long have you been in Diamond Creek?" Cammi asked.

Having been new in this small town myself, I knew the minute a new face appeared, unless it was obviously a tourist, people wanted the entire life story.

Gemma smiled. "Just a month. Hopefully I'll see some of you at class next week."

I wanted to ask Cammi to ride with me. When Susie pointed out that her small truck was crowded because Tess ended up needing a ride too, I wanted to kiss her. Susie was seriously nosy and had a reputation for interfering. I didn't mind one bit if she was interfering and trying to make sure Cammi needed to ride with someone else.

"You can ride with me," I offered.

When Cammi's eyes swung to meet mine, I felt that now familiar jolt of lust sizzle down my spine. A few minutes later, we were in my truck. I came to the conclusion it probably hadn't been the best plan to christen my truck the way we did. Because now all I could think about was finding another secluded location and getting my hands all over her.

I would have to make do with much less. "Come here," I murmured, reaching for her hand and giving it a little tug.

She unbuckled her seatbelt and slid to the middle, immediately buckling up again. Because Cammi was a buckle up kind of girl.

"Close enough?" she asked.

"Yep. It feels good to have you beside me."

The moment I said that, I realized the potential implications. The crazy thing was, instead of freaking out, I experienced the mental and emotional equivalent of a shrug. Although it was hard to miss Cammi tensing slightly beside me. Seeing as we were about to meet our friends in a matter of minutes, I knew now wasn't the time to ask what she might be worrying about. Instead, I slid my hand on her thigh because I couldn't help myself.

Chapter Twenty-Four

CAMMI

For the second time in a matter of weeks, I was at an actual social occasion with Elias, and he was behaving as if we were a *real* thing. I knew I needed to maybe ask him what it was that we were doing. Because it was awfully hard not to fall for him. He was the most ridiculously tempting man I'd ever been with. He was the kind of man women ruined panties over on the regular.

I tried to ignore Susie's way too satisfied look. Tess even nudged her in the side at one point. Tess was a more protective friend. To clarify, Susie was crazy protective but more interfering.

"I think you're smart to just stick with the menu they have," Daphne was saying from my side. "Get settled and figure out the flow of everything and then call me. I'll help you brainstorm."

I looked toward her. "Daphne, you're a real chef. I don't have money to pay you for that right now. I'm not sure how fancy I want to be either."

Daphne regarded me quietly, her eyes softening. "Cammi, we're friends and you can bounce ideas off of me. I occasionally make more high-end things, but there's nothing I respect more than really well done simple food. I love Misty Mountain Café, although your coffee is better," she added quickly, "but their menu is pretty basic. I think it'd be great for you to bring the food up to the level of your coffee."

"Yes!" Susie chimed in from across the table as she lifted up her glass of water.

"If you make food as good as your coffee, I'll be there every morning. I won't feel guilty either because I won't be skipping your coffee," Diego explained.

I experienced a flash of pride. I had yet to succeed on the food front, but I was feeling hopeful. No matter what, I loved having such loyal customers.

Conversation moved along, and I savored the feel of Elias's arm resting across my shoulders. Occasionally, his thumb traced an idle caress along my collarbone and it felt like a lick of fire over my skin. When I said women ruined panties over him, I wasn't exaggerating, not even a little. Mine were already ruined for the night.

Flynn had signaled for the check when I felt Elias tense. The man was all muscle, so it was pretty hard to miss when his arm went tight over my shoulders. I glanced up toward him. Following his gaze, I noticed a woman approaching the table. I watched as Diego cast a quick look at Elias, his eyes hardening when he looked toward the woman.

Even from across the room, I could tell she was beautiful. She had glossy, straight blond hair. She was one of those women who tended to make me feel a little frumpy. I was always in a rush and usually pulled my hair back and swiped lip gloss on before running out, and that was when I was trying. This woman was perfectly put together, outfitted in a pair of jeans and a blouse that must've been ironed. She even wore smart-looking heels, which clicked on the floor.

She stopped beside our table, looking right at Elias before her eyes flicked to Flynn and Diego. "Hello," she said simply.

Elias barely moved. His arm was practically a board on my shoulders at this point. His voice was tight and controlled when he spoke. "Hello, Sandra."

Diego and Flynn stayed silent.

"I was hoping I could talk to you," she added.

"Nothing to say," Elias said.

"Elias, please—" she pressed.

Flynn cut in. "What would you need to say after five years?"

Those of us who didn't know what was going on were quiet but definitely alert.

"Flynn, if you don't mind, this is really none of your business," the woman added.

Diego spoke next. Diego who was always kind, big hearted, and easy-going was anything but in this moment. "Of course, it's our business. You fucked over our friend. And frankly, made it all worse because it was with his friend. I'd say that's enough betrayal, don't you think? You made your preferences clear."

I had to give it to this woman, she didn't even flinch. Her eyes took on a hard look. "I would still like to speak to Elias."

Elias leaned over and whispered in my ear, "Because I don't want this to become more of a scene, I'm gonna go." He kissed me quickly on the cheek and stood. "I'll deal with it."

I watched him leave with my stomach twisting in sick knots.

Chapter Twenty-Five

ELIAS

"What the hell do you want, Sandra?" I asked.

After leaving the brewery, Sandra tried to persuade me to ride with her, but that was a hard pass on my part. She'd followed me to Sally's, another bar in Diamond Creek. It wasn't because I wanted to be at a bar, but I didn't want to meet with her anywhere that wasn't completely public. Cammi had looked like she was freaking right the fuck out. I kind of was too, to be honest. But for the moment, I had no choice, but to deal with this situation.

Sally's was hopping. Like the brewery, it was a local favorite hang-out. It was in an old barn with a full bar and music stage on one side for small bands, and a restaurant with pub fare on the other. We were seated at a small table right by the door. I intended to be out of here as soon as I figured out what the hell Sandra was doing here. Alaska wasn't exactly in her neck of the woods. Last I'd known, she was still in the Air Force and stationed in California.

I looked across the table, and felt nothing. Sandra

was attractive in a sharp-edged way. She had a willowy build and cornflower blond hair. Her brown eyes tilted at the corners, and her face was all clean angles. I wondered what I'd ever seen in her. Oh, she was beautiful, all right, but I felt nothing anymore.

They say people change, and I supposed I'd definitely changed from back when I was involved with her. Although, the way things ended with us would sour most people on romance.

She looked tense. Her shoulders hitched up slightly and her jaw clenched as she looked at me from across the table. "How are you, Elias?"

"I'm fine, Sandra. Cut to the chase. I know you didn't come here for some kind of reunion because I'm pretty sure you know that's impossible. What do you need?"

"Geez, Elias. Are you still angry with me?" she countered, the hint of bitterness in her tone startling me.

She was the one who screwed me over, so I didn't get that. I took a breath, letting it out as I did an internal scan. "No," I finally replied. "I'm not angry. I hope life is treating you well, but I'm not interested in trying to have a friendship with you."

I was furious at the way Sandra showed up, because I knew it looked suspicious to Cammi and that was the last thing Cammi needed. Trust didn't come easy to her for obvious reasons. I would have to contemplate just why I was so concerned about that at another time. I'd gone from trying to ignore my attraction to Cammi to diving into it so deeply that my denial wasn't helpful anymore. I knew it was far more than simple physical desire at play.

Sandra swallowed and unclasped her hands to take

a sip of her water. "Understood. I kind of have a big ask."

A subtle tingle of trepidation chased down my spine. "Uh, okay. What's that?"

"I have a son. He's um—"

I felt abruptly sick when she paused to take another swallow of water. "You're telling me this now? If you fucking tell me I have a son and you didn't tell me about it, I don't even know what I'm gonna do," I said flatly.

"He's not yours. I swear," she said quickly. "Greg's the father."

I nodded slowly. "So, it's his son then. Still not sure why you're here to see me."

Betrayal was a strange thing. It could cut so deep. I didn't wish I had a child with Sandra, but I couldn't help but wonder if the man I'd once considered a close friend had known he had a son on the way. That was another secret he kept from me and the rest of our tight circle of friends.

Sandra took a shaky breath, unaware of my mental machinations. "If you recall, those last months before Greg died, you and I didn't see each other because we weren't in the same place."

Her voice cracked a little there, and I couldn't even feel satisfaction at the possible twinge of guilt she was experiencing. Apparently, she hadn't found it worth traveling to see me, but somehow, she and Greg had managed to make time to see each other. Considering he was stationed with me, well, that burned a little. I was over Sandra, but being betrayed by a good friend still stung. I didn't want it to hurt, but loyalty mattered to me.

"I recall."

"Mathematically, it just doesn't add up. There's no way you're the father. I always knew that," she finally said.

"Math comes in handy sometimes," I said slowly. "Why are you here, Sandra? I'm still confused about that."

"Because Greg's family is disputing his paternity." She took a shaky breath. "He knew I was pregnant." She paused here, her eyes searching mine. I didn't know what she saw there. "I know it doesn't matter now, but I was going to tell you what happened between Greg and me. I just wanted to do it face to face. I thought you deserved that."

I absorbed her words and was relieved to discover I didn't feel any fresh burst of anger. I was well past being angry with her. I gave a light shrug. "It's okay. We can't change what happened. I appreciate that you meant to tell me."

"Elias, I'm—"

I shook my head, not interested in furthering this branch of the conversation. "Tell me why you're here."

She took a shaky breath before continuing. "Like I said, Greg knew I was pregnant. I told him as soon as I found out. I don't want to create problems, but money is tight, and our son qualifies for his survivor benefits. Greg's family doesn't want me to have that, so they're taking me to court. Since he's not alive, and I had no formal relationship to him, like we weren't married or anything, I don't have any way to get a genetic sample to prove he's Greg's son. My attorney recommended that I talk with you so we can rule you out as a father. They're arguing that they believe you're the father."

Her words came out with a few starts and stops,

and I actually felt a stab of sympathy for her. She looked absolutely miserable trying to explain this to me. Much as I wasn't a fan of my old friend and certainly didn't appreciate what happened, it was bullshit what his family was trying to do. "I'll take a paternity test. I'm going to assume you're confident about the results."

"I am," she said quickly. "His date of birth is April seventh, and he just turned five this year."

I was good at math. I didn't remember many dates, but I hadn't forgotten the date my old friend died. His son's birthday was exactly four months and one week after his death. Sandra was right. We hadn't been together physically for over five months by that point.

Actually seeing Sandra clarified for me that I was more than over her. Yet, the burn of my old friend's betrayal was still there. Being apart for chunks of time when you were in the military was part of the deal sometimes. The lingering sense of betrayal was connected to my friend, not her. Sadly, she didn't even know she wasn't the only friend Greg had betrayed, but that wasn't my story to tell.

"I assume we could do that locally," I added.

She let out a giant breath. "Oh, thank you, Elias." She pressed a palm to her chest.

"It's no problem. If Greg was the father, his will should be honored."

"I already found out we can just do the paternity test at the hospital here. It's Alaska, so nothing's fast. Apparently, they send it up to a lab in Anchorage, it's five days for processing. I'm staying in a hotel here. We can do it tomorrow if that works for you."

"I'll make it work. I prefer to do it in the morning because I need to fly in the afternoon."

"Whatever works for you. The lab said you can drop in. Just go when it works for you."

"You got it. Now, if you don't mind, I need to go." I stood from the table, and she stood with me.

"I don't have any reason to stay," she said when I glanced toward her. We exited out into the parking lot. "It's beautiful here." She looked up toward the sky.

"It is," I said simply.

The moon was rising over the mountains in the distance, claiming the sky from the lingering colors of the sunset. A smudgy lavender, early night sky was taking over from the last trails of pink and red left behind by the sun.

"Elias, I just want to say that I'm really sorry. I can't say I never should've been with Greg, but I never should've done it the way I did. I can't imagine what that feels like for you because he was your friend. I know it doesn't help, at all, but he felt terrible too."

I absorbed that. "I know. It is what it is. I'm glad you came and asked me for this. I hate it when people do shit like that. No matter what happened between Greg and me, I know he would want his son taken care of."

Maybe I hadn't expected my friend to do what he did, but I did know that. "You doing okay?" I asked, actually meaning it and hoping she was okay.

Sandra nodded. "I am. I really am. I'll definitely let you know when we get the results."

"As you said, the math already rules me out, so I'm not worried about that. You take care, all right?"

She reached over, placing her palm on my arm and squeezing gently, her touch cool. "You too. Now, go find that girl you were with. I'm sure she might be confused about me showing up like that. If you need me to clear up anything, just say the word."

"Thanks. Night, Sandra." I lifted my hand in a wave as I walked away and climbed in my truck. I started it, aiming toward Cammi's house. I needed to talk to her.

Unfortunately, she wasn't there when I stopped by and didn't answer my texts, or my call.

Chapter Twenty-Six

CAMMI

"Ugh," I muttered.

I lay still in bed, a little afraid to move too abruptly because my head was pounding. I prayed, irrationally, that my alarm was wrong. Maybe it *was* wrong. I knew that was highly unlikely, considering it was my smartphone and it was an auto-set alarm. I'd been getting up every day at that time and had for years when my coffee truck was open.

I opened one eye. Glimmers of light were coming in through the windows. With a sigh, I opened the other eye and experimentally moved my head as I reached to pick up my phone and check the time.

No shock, but my alarm wasn't wrong. My head was definitely not happy about moving.

I sat up slowly and trudged into the bathroom, setting my phone on the counter by the sink. Blessedly, my on-demand hot water heater responded to my demand and hot water cascaded out of the showerhead in seconds. I downed two ibuprofen and climbed in the shower.

After Elias had unceremoniously left with a woman

that I later learned was his ex-girlfriend, Diego and Flynn had assured me Elias had no lingering feelings for her. They wanted to make sure I had nothing to worry about. Of course, that didn't alleviate my mortification. Elias and I couldn't even define what we were, and now his ex was showing up for some mysterious reason. I didn't like mysteries.

Aside from that, if I hadn't already been painfully aware of my issues with trust, my brain had gone into anxiety overtime last night. I figured Elias must've been hiding something from me and from his friends. Why else would his ex-girlfriend come all the way to Alaska? Alaska wasn't exactly on the way to anywhere unless you've lived here.

After the guys had left, Susie and Tess stayed with me and provided moral support, along with extra margaritas.

Fuck my life. Maybe I needed to just focus on work. I sure had plenty to focus on. Just yesterday afternoon, the bank called and said the sellers were willing to close early if I was ready to take over the reins. Apparently, the owner's mother had taken a turn for the worse, and they wanted to leave as soon as possible.

Maybe I felt a little overwhelmed by all of it, but I could handle the coffee part with no trouble. The sale included keeping their current staff, knowing that some of them could leave if they chose anyway. All in all, the café was on auto pilot if I didn't make any changes except for the coffee. It would mean work and lots of it, but I could use the distraction.

After my shower, I made some coffee thinking that would help even more with my hangover, although first I made myself drink a full glass of water. Once I was dressed, I texted the lady at the bank and let her know we could close by this weekend if they wanted. That gave me three days. I could totally use being so busy I didn't have time to think.

I raced into the coffee truck, planning to handle the morning rush and then head over to Misty Mountain Café for a quick planning session with the employees who were about to become my staff inside of three days.

"Morning," Amy said when she banged open the door to the truck a few minutes after I'd arrived.

My head felt as if a hammer had struck it, but I took a breath and another swallow of coffee. My headache was gradually starting to fade.

"Morning," I said in return. "Here's your five dollars." I turned back and handed over the change to the woman in line.

Amy had her apron on in no time and took over with customers while I made coffees. The less talking for me, the better.

During a very brief lull, Amy asked in a low voice, "Cammi, are you okay?"

I cast her a glare. "I don't look that bad."

She held both hands up in apology. "You don't look that bad, but you look, I don't know... Not good?"

I reached to the small cabinet above where we were working where I had a mini first aid kit. I fished out some more ibuprofen. "My head's killing me, but it's getting better."

More customers arrived, and we carried on. I was beyond grateful Amy was such a good employee. She picked up my slack easily.

Then, the dreaded moment happened. "Hey, Cammi."

Of course, Elias just *had* to come by this morning. This shouldn't have surprised me, and it didn't really. I supposed I'd kind of been hoping he wouldn't stop by for coffee for once.

I tried something resembling a smile when I lifted my head and kept my eyes carefully level. "Hi," I said, relieved I had coffees to make to keep my hands busy.

"Elias's usual," Amy said.

My heart twisted in my chest and emotion knotted in my throat. I suddenly hated that I knew exactly what Elias's usual was. I knew how to make it so he loved it and came here every day. Even before we had crazy, hot sex.

I worked in silence, but his presence was nearly impossible to ignore. I felt like a tuning fork, tuned solely to the frequency of him. That subtle vibration and awareness hummed through my body.

When I had his coffee ready, I snapped the lid on and passed it over the counter, lifting my head just briefly to catch his gaze waiting. My heart twisted again, and I smiled even though my face felt like it might crack. "There you go."

"Do you have a few minutes?" he asked.

"Not really."

At least I wasn't lying about that. Amy was already calling over the next order. Elias looked at me for a long moment. "Don't worry about what happened last night. It was nothing that has anything to do with you. I promise."

I did that weird smiling thing again, my face feeling stiff. "It's okay. You don't owe me any explanations. I really do need to keep working."

He hesitated and then nodded. "I'll be by later."

I could tell Amy was wondering just what we were talking about, but we were blessedly very busy for the next hour. When there was finally a break, she said, "I hope you didn't break up with Elias."

I whipped my eyes toward her, relieved my headache appeared to be gone because moving that fast didn't feel like another hammer striking my head. "We were never officially together, so I can't break up with him. We just went on a date or two," I muttered, not about to get into the details of the incredible sex we had with my employee. I did have some boundaries.

"He really likes you," she said, resting her hand on her hip.

"Amy, not now, okay?"

The universe was on my side because another group of customers appeared. I skipped out a little while later, leaving Amy in charge of closing up while I headed over to Misty Mountain Café. I was still debating if I was going to keep the name. It didn't sit right to call the café Red Truck Coffee when it wasn't in a truck.

Chapter Twenty-Seven

CAMMI

"What are you talking about?" I asked Susie, a little exasperated with her.

"Elias was at the hospital yesterday morning. So was that woman who showed up at the brewery."

"Her name is Sandra," I forced out. Maybe I didn't know her, but it felt weird to refer to her as "that woman" over and over again.

"Why are you telling me this?" I adjusted the phone between my ear and shoulder and nudged a stack of clean towels in place by the espresso machine in my coffee truck.

"I called Violet," Susie explained.

Now I was more confused. "What? What does Violet have to do with this?"

"She knows why Elias was there. He was in the lab."

I couldn't help myself. "What did Violet say?"

Susie let out an aggrieved sigh. "She won't tell me anything! She said she has to protect confidentiality. She wouldn't even acknowledge he was there. Which is ridiculous because I was there in the waiting room at the same freaking time, and she saw us both. It's like she wants me to pretend I didn't see him."

Violet Hamilton worked in the lab at the hospital and was a friend. We all knew her well, and she was awesome.

"Well, would you want her just telling people why you were there? Come to think of it, why were you there?" I asked.

"Oh, no biggie," Susie said. "Just my annual numbers thing where they check cholesterol and all that. Elias was in and out super-fast, and Sandra was there before him only to fill out paperwork. She was gone by the time he got there if you were wondering."

I totally was, but I wasn't going to fess up to it. "This isn't really helping," I pointed out.

"Oh, I'm sorry," Susie said. "They weren't there together. He looked kinda down and told me to tell you he wants to talk to you. Are you ignoring his texts and calls?"

"So what if I am?" I mumbled. "I'm busy, and I think that's for the best right now. I already had one round of finding out some kind of major stuff a guy was hiding from me. Elias and I weren't even that serious, and I just don't think I'm ready for a relationship. Maybe it's not a big deal, but I'm freaking out, and I need to get a grip."

I could sense Susie's frustration through the phone line. "Sweetie, just—"

"Susie, I know you mean well, and I love you for it. But I need to not be freaking out right now. I really can't do this. I've gotta go. I promise we'll talk later.

I hung up the phone and sat down on an overturned plastic bucket with a hefty sigh. Tears were stinging my eyes, and I was tired. I was legitimately tired, but I also knew I was right. I needed some time to gather myself together, mentally and emotionally. I *was* going to talk to Elias when I was ready. But I couldn't rush into it. I was basically losing my shit over this. I was already falling in love with someone else. Why, oh why, did Elias have to be the kind of guy that I fell for so freaking fast? This was way worse than with any other guy.

Of course, now I couldn't help but wonder why Elias went to the hospital lab. My brain went right to the obvious possibility—a paternity test. Resting my elbows on my knees, I looked around my little coffee truck. Despite my emotional tumult, a weary smile curled my lips. I loved this little space. It was all mine, and I was so proud of what I'd done. I was a little anxious—okay, maybe more like losing-sleep kind of anxious—about my new business. Yet, I thought perhaps I was up to the challenge.

It was early, earlier than I usually got here. Like me, Susie was an early morning worker, so she'd known I'd be up when she called. I stood from the plastic bucket and tapped the keyboard to power up my laptop. I quickly made a few orders for supplies here and checked my email to see if the sellers had sent over their stock status yet. They were lining up supply orders for the next two months so that I could walk into this with things ready to roll. With Susie's firm guidance, we'd made sure that was part of the contract. There was nothing from them in my email yet, but it was still early.

I wasn't ready to open yet, but I decided an early morning cleaning was always a worthwhile activity, so I settled in to get the place spotless. I was going to need to hire someone else to help over here. No matter how things shook out in the long term as far as where I put my energy, for getting started I knew I needed to put more time over in the new business.

I heard gravel under tires and hoped whoever it was had enough sense to see I wasn't officially open. Many locals knew my vehicle, so they might make assumptions about that.

I had emptied out one of my small storage cabinets and was re-organizing the supplies, pulling forward the older items and so on, when there was a light knock on the back door where I came in. That indicated it was likely someone who knew me.

Taking a deep breath, I wiped my hands on my apron and strode to the back of the truck to open the narrow door. Peering out, I found Elias standing there.

My heart gave a spinning kick in my chest and set off at a galloping beat. I could see tiny flecks of amber in his chocolate eyes in the gray light of dawn. His hair was a little damp. He wore a navy-blue T-shirt over a pair of faded black jeans and his usual well-worn leather boots. Gah! Why did he have to be so yummy looking? I swallowed and took a shallow breath.

"Hey," he said simply.

"Hey," I squeaked, my voice cracking on that single syllable.

"Can I come in?"

I opened my mouth to say "no" when there was a rustling sound outside, to the side of the truck and out of view for me. Elias stepped back quickly, leaning around the door. Following that, there was a faster shuffling sound, moving in the direction of the trees to the side of my small gravel parking area.

Elias was smiling when his stepped back. "Your little buddy is around."

"My little buddy?"

"The porcupine. Maybe you should give him a name."

I couldn't help my smile, my lips tugging up in reflex. Then, of course, I recalled Elias helping me chase the porcupine out of my coffee truck that night, the very night when he first kissed me.

"I'll have to think on a name. Come on in," I said, gesturing him inside.

The air was cool outside, and it was getting chilly inside with the door open. Elias stepped past me, and I closed the door, just standing there for a second. My space that felt cozy and comforting was suddenly filled with his presence. He was a tall man and exuded that raw, easy masculinity.

There wasn't too much room in here, and he leaned his hips against the narrow counter on the wall opposite the serving window.

"Would you like some coffee?" I asked as I quickly stepped to where I'd been working and finished returning the items to the small cabinet to the side of my beloved espresso machine.

"I wasn't gonna ask, but since you offered, absolutely."

I took a swallow of my own coffee before beginning to prep his. He was quiet for just long enough that the tension in my neck and chest started to ease.

"So, can I explain what happened the other night?"

My muscles tightened again. I took a breath and replied, "You don't owe me any explanations, Elias."

I tapped the button to start his double shot and turned, curling my arms around my waist as I rested my hips against the serving counter. He reached across the narrow space, his hand lightly catching my elbow. When he slid his palm down my forearm, I reflexively unwound my arms. He lightly held my hand in his, his thumb brushing back and forth along the sensitive skin on the inside of my wrist as he looked at me intently.

"I do."

I started to shake my head and was mortified to feel tears stinging in my eyes again. I swallowed, the sound audible in the small space.

"Maybe we didn't plan this, and maybe we haven't really talked about what's happening, but something is happening for us. I would never, *never*, see anyone behind your back," he said, his voice low and intent.

I blinked away my tears and nodded. The espresso machine beeped, and he dropped my hand as I spun away. He was quiet while I got his coffee ready. After I handed it to him, I curled my hands over the edge of the counter while he took a sip.

His lips kicked up at one corner, sending butterflies wild in my belly. "Delicious. As always."

I could hear the tick of the clock mounted above the door as his eyes searched my face before he continued, "Sandra and I haven't been together since before I came to Alaska. That was five years ago, in case you were counting. I found out she was seeing one of my closest friends behind my back. The whole thing was a mess because I didn't find out until after that same friend died in an accident. I'm pretty sure we'd have broken up sooner, but I was on duty and we weren't even in the same location."

My hand flew to my chest. "That's awful. I'm so sorry."

He dipped his chin in acknowledgment and took another swallow of coffee. "It sucked and was kind of a mindfuck for me. Obviously, it was bad for my girlfriend to screw around on me, but what he did felt worse. He was as tight with me as any of my other friends. Or, I thought he was. You know Flynn, Diego, Tucker, and Gabriel, we all were together in the Air Force. Greg was one of us."

"I'm really sorry," I offered again. It made me want to wind back time and tell Sandra how foolish she'd been to hurt a man like Elias.

He held my eyes for a moment before continuing, "Things were hard for me after Greg died. I wasn't in the accident with him, but I was one of the responders and got injured." He paused, taking a gulp of his coffee and closing his eyes. When they opened again, the look there was weary. "It didn't last long, but I got hooked on painkillers in the aftermath." His gaze searched mine, and I sensed he was trying to assess my reaction.

My heart squeezed, and I wanted to cry. My emotions were on edge as it was, and I was tired. I managed to keep it together. "That's awful. If you're worried I might think something about that, don't. The problems with painkillers are all over the news. Is it difficult for you now?"

He shook his head swiftly. "No, it's not. I mean, I'm ashamed, but lucky for me, it was short-lived. My doctor then told me the longer it lasts, the more your body adjusts, which makes it harder to kick."

I managed a breath, thinking that I couldn't even imagine how hard it had been for him to learn his friend had betrayed him, and be dealing with injuries and pain. "I'm glad you're okay," I whispered.

"I am. I really am. If you ever need to ask more about it, you can."

My heart was kicking in my chest. He was talking as if there was a future for us, like I might want to ask him about this. My emotions felt all jumbled, so I just nodded.

"So back to the other night. Obviously, I didn't expect to see my ex. She's here because she got pregnant before my friend died. I know it's not my son because the math doesn't add up. She was pretty direct about that. Anyway, Greg knew about it, and their son's entitled to his survivor's benefits. Apparently, his family is disputing it. They're claiming I'm the father, so I agreed to do a paternity test to show that's not the case."

I really, *really* wanted to believe Elias. It wasn't that I thought he was lying. I didn't. I was just tired of myself and my stupid issues with trust. I didn't want to be caught up in this tangled mess that wasn't even mine.

"Okay," I said slowly before reaching for my coffee and taking a big gulp. "You really didn't have to tell me all this."

Elias searched my eyes, and I wanted to look away. I didn't.

"Cammi, I get after what happened to you and your last relationship it could've looked like I was hiding something. That's why I'm telling you this. I wasn't. I didn't even know Sandra was pregnant when Greg died."

I cleared my throat, wishing it didn't feel so tight with emotion. "I appreciate that, but it's not like you've made any promises. I don't even know if we're in a relationship. And, I'm not holding you responsible for that not being clear," I added hurriedly.

"Are we okay?" he pressed.

"Sure. Sorry about what you went through."

I knew my responses were curt and not really helpful, but I didn't know how to handle this, much less what to say.

He lifted a shoulder in a light shrug. "We all go through hard things. It's part of life, I suppose."

I nodded, because that was obviously true. After another few beats of quiet, he said, "So, maybe things have been vague, but this isn't just a fling for me."

I stared at him, hope beating out a little tap dance inside of my heart. "Um, ok-aaay, but it's not like we expected this. I mean, you *did* kind of try to steer clear of me for years. That's what you said," I mumbled uncertainly.

I felt as if I were stumbling and tripping inside, not sure how to navigate this conversation at all.

Elias reached for my hand again. His grip was warm, and I wanted to burst into tears and fall into his arms. But, I absolutely didn't want to be that foolish.

"Yeah, so maybe I did try to steer clear. Now that I told you how my last relationship went, maybe you can understand I was a little gun shy and a lot bitter. Maybe I didn't let myself think about it, but I knew there was a chance I would fall hard for you. It's turned out to be more than a chance."

My heart was knocking hard in my chest, and I really didn't know how to handle any of this. "I do understand but I'm a little confused right now." I paused, swallowing, trying to push through the logjam of emotion in my throat. It ached. "I'm not sure what the best thing is for me. This whole thing with your ex freaked me out more than I expected, and I need to figure some things out for myself," I explained haltingly. "And, I'm really busy. I'm closing early on the loan for Misty Mountain."

Ugh. This was awful. I didn't know what to think or do, and here I was talking about being freaking busy.

Elias's eyes searched mine, and it felt like he was

trying to climb inside my heart. I wanted to close the shutters on all the windows of my battered heart and hide.

"You're busy?" His eyes were warm and understanding, and it only made me feel worse than I already did.

"Yeah." My voice came out in a cracked whisper.

"Okay, sweetheart." His thumb brushed along my wrist before he released my hand. "I'll wait until you're ready."

Just then, the sound of tires on gravel reached us, and I glanced at the clock. My official opening time was only one minute away. He pushed away from the counter and dipped his head to brush a kiss across my lips. The brief point of contact sent electricity sizzling through me.

"I'll be in touch. You can call me whenever you need me."

With that, Elias left and I sat down on that plastic bucket again and gave myself one minute to cry. I opened five minutes late because one minute wasn't enough.

Chapter Twenty-Eight

ELIAS

"Thank you," Sandra said through the phone line.

"It was really no problem," I replied, pausing to stuff my jacket in my backpack as I got ready to leave the plane hangar for the evening.

"I know you aren't the father, and I'll call as soon as we have the official results."

"I hope this helps resolve the problems with Greg's family."

"It should." There was a pause, and Sandra cleared her throat. "I know it's been a while, and I can't change the past, but I want you to know I'm sorry again."

"Apology accepted," I replied, meaning it. I *had* let go of what happened with Sandra, and perhaps I would always be a little bitter about my old friend's involvement, but we all do stupid shit.

"Now, I hope you won't let that hold you back from finding the right girl. Are you serious about that woman I saw you with?" she asked.

I thought about Cammi—her blue eyes, the way she somehow carried the subtle scent of flowers, her toughness underneath her sweetness, and the way it felt to hold her in my arms. "Yeah, I am."

"Well then, I know you're a good man, so take good care of her."

With that, we ended the call, and I headed over to yoga class. When I drove by Misty Mountain Café and saw Cammi's SUV, I resisted the urge to turn in and see how things were going. It had only been a few days, and I knew she needed space, so fucking dammit, I was going to give it to her.

The other afternoon, I'd gone to get another massage, consciously hoping that maybe, just maybe, Cammi would be there again. She wasn't. The man who gave me the massage did a great job, but he was no Cammi. I was on my way to yoga now because Flynn asked us to go again. I didn't mind, but it was fucking hysterical that Daphne had persuaded him to keep going to yoga classes.

Once again, I couldn't help but be hopeful that perhaps Cammi would be there. No such luck. The yoga class was good, and I got to enjoy the sideshow of Diego struggling not to ogle the yoga teacher.

"Dude," I whispered where I stood beside him. "She said to look forward."

"Fuck you," he muttered under his breath.

"I don't think that's very fitting right now," I countered.

"Everything okay over here?" Gemma asked when she paused beside Diego.

"Yeah, Diego just had a question about the posture," I offered. I couldn't resist giving him a little hell.

Actually, maybe it was a favor. Because then Gemma helped him adjust into the posture in question. After class, we all headed back to the resort. It was a card night. Perhaps that wasn't the best fit after yoga, but it was always good to chill out with my friends.

After a dinner that involved some kind of coconut Thai curry that Daphne whipped up, we decamped to the private apartment Flynn shared with Daphne and Cat.

"Where's Cat?" I asked as I flopped down on one side of their sectional sofa.

"She's spending the night with a friend," Daphne called over. Diego sat down at an angle near me and Gabriel on the other end of the sectional. We were all beat this evening. It had been a busy few days of flying.

Flynn walked into the kitchen area, stopping beside Daphne to drop a kiss on the side of her neck. She smiled up at him. "I made you guys fresh brownies."

"Sweet!" Diego called as he pumped his fist in the air.

"Please tell me there's vanilla ice cream to go with them," Tucker said as he sat down.

"Absolutely."

"Did you make that too?" Tucker added dryly.

Daphne crossed over to rest her hands on her hips as she surveyed us where she stood by the coffee table. "I could, but I didn't have time."

"Where are you headed?" Flynn asked as she stepped into her clogs by the door.

Daphne glanced back. "Y'all are having your boys' card night, so I'm going over to Nora's cabin. We're gonna have a girls' night. We need more girls."

"My sister's coming next summer," Tucker called.

"Awesome. That'll make three of us, and there's

still six of you," she said just as Grant stepped through the door.

"Six of who?" he asked.

"Boys who call themselves men," Daphne teased. "All right, I'm outta here. Have fun." She slipped through the door with a wave at the room in general.

Not much later, the entire pan of brownies and the entire gallon of ice cream were gone. In our defense, there were six full-grown men.

I leaned back in the corner of the sectional, resting my leg on it and experimentally rotating my foot.

"How's it feel?" Diego asked from my side.

"Decent. I'll take it. I don't think I'll ever be one hundred percent. When I get old, I'll probably be able to gauge whether or not it's gonna rain by this ankle, but it works."

Diego chuckled as he set down his cards. "Any word?" he asked

"Word about what?" Grant chimed in from where he sat organizing his hand of cards.

I sighed. "You haven't heard yet?"

"Heard what? I've been up in Anchorage for the last four days."

"My ex showed up, and I had to do a paternity test. Don't worry, there's no chance I'm the father. It's not official yet though," I added when Grant's eyes went comically wide.

"Not to sound stupid, but if there's no chance you're the father, why the hell did you have to do a paternity test? And what are you actually talking about?"

Flynn chuckled from where he sat beside Grant. Grant didn't even know me when I'd been seeing Sandra.

"It's old news. I needed to do the paternity test

because the actual father died, but his family is disputing paternity because they don't want her to get his survivor benefits. They claim I'm the father, and I'm not."

Grant only looked more confused. I felt compelled to explain further. "It's complicated. She was screwing around on me, I broke up with her, but she was already pregnant with the other guy's kid when all that went down. That's all."

Grant took a long drag from his beer. He let out a sigh and shook his head. "Dude, you're doing her a solid. After she screwed around on you, I don't know if I could've done that."

I shrugged. "Maybe. Shit happens. It's not my kid, but I think it's bullshit to keep the kid from getting survivor benefits. That only hurts the innocent party in all this."

"When will you know?" Tucker piped up.

"Violet at the lab said probably five days. She told me it could be sooner but she didn't want to make any promises because they have to send the samples up to the lab in Anchorage. I'm hoping to hear soon."

"How is Cammi?" Flynn asked, his assessing gaze holding mine.

Gabriel played a winning hand before I answered. Flynn started to shuffle, because apparently that was his permanent job these days, before he prompted me again. "About Cammi?"

"We're on pause. I guess," I replied.

"Did she freak out about Sandra showing up like that?" Gabriel asked.

"Sorta. I think she understands the details now, but she said she needed a little space, so I'm trying to give it to her."

The game moved along, and other conversations

picked up. Diego looked over at one point and offered, "You're not asking, but I'm not sure if you let Cammi know how you feel."

"What do you mean?" A little hum of anxiety churned in my gut.

Diego gave me a long look. "Dude, it's obvious to me you're falling for her in a big way. I guess she asked for a break, and I think it's good to give her a little breathing room. You tend to play your cards seriously close to your chest. Evidence for how often you win when you're in the mood. But, now is not the time to play things cool."

If there was a heartbeat in our tight group of friends, it was Diego. He was the emotional core of our group and intensely loyal. I didn't doubt that if and when he ever fell for anyone, it would be like a ton of bricks falling from the sky.

"I'm not playing it cool. I told her I thought we had something," I insisted.

Diego rolled his eyes, and Flynn must've heard the end of that. "Dude, saying you "have something" is the kind of thing people say when they're fishing around for dates on those apps. You're about to go up in flames with Cammi whenever you're near her. I think you need to do a little bit more than say you think you have "something"." He emphasized his point with air quotes around something.

Diego chuckled, lifting his chin toward Flynn in acknowledgment. "My point exactly."

Chapter Twenty-Nine

ELIAS

The following morning, I was out prepping a plane for a flight. It was an all mail delivery today for me. Nora usually handled most of the scheduling and did a good job of changing it up for us. Some days were tourist days and other days we got to fly the gorgeous skies of Alaska with nothing but the sound of the plane engine and the mountains to keep us company while we dropped off various deliveries.

My phone vibrated in my pocket, and I fished it out to glance down at the screen. It was a text from Sandra. *Results are in: you're not the father. I already knew that, but I thought you'd want to know for sure.*

I tapped out a quick reply to Sandra. *Thanks for letting me know and hope that helps. You take care now.*

Just then, my phone rang, and I saw it was the hospital number. I only knew this because I had entered it as a contact in my phone in the aftermath of my recovery after the accident last winter.

"Hello," I answered.

"May I please speak with Elias?"

"Hey, Violet. I recognize your voice," I said. "I'm

guessing you're calling me with the results. I already heard."

She laughed. "You're not the father, but then that's what you said. I guess it's none of my business, but I admit to being nosy about your situation."

I chuckled. "No big deal. You can be nosy. It was a blast from the past, and a custody case where they're trying to deny child support and say I was the father. We didn't end on great terms before, but it's not right for people to pull that kind of shit, so I did the deed. Or rather, I didn't do the deed."

Violet's laugh rang out in my ear. "You're a good man, Elias. I'll see you around. Don't forget, you know where to find me if you need to get your cheek swabbed or some blood drawn."

"I sure do. You take care, Violet. Give Sawyer my best," I said, referring to her husband.

"You got it. I gotta go 'cause I'm getting paged. See ya."

I hung up my phone and slid it in my pocket. Another second later, I pulled it back out. I typed out a quick text to Cammi.

Just wanted you to know the results came back, only confirming what I already knew. I'm not a surprise father. I hope you're doing okay. Miss you.

I'd gone by reliably to get my coffee at Red Truck Coffee. Although I was giving her space, I thought it would be weird for me not to do what I'd done for years. Out of those mornings, I'd only seen her twice. According to Amy, Cammi was busy over at Misty Mountain Café most days.

As I flew into the blue sky a few minutes later, I pondered Diego's and Flynn's pointed comments last night. I suppose I did play my cards close. It felt fucking monumental to tell Cammi I knew we had something. Yet, after what she'd been through, she had her own reasons for being doubtful about that.

I was unloading the delivery for a small village onto the pallets set up when Stan, whose last name I didn't even know, rolled up on his four-wheeler, a common form of transportation in the smaller villages in Alaska. He ran the grocery store and cast me a quick smile. "What do we have today?"

"A shit ton of food," I replied with a wry grin.

Stan chuckled and cut the engine on his four-wheeler, climbing off and quickly helping me unload. Stan used to be the chief of the small tribe for this village. He was older now and told me he enjoyed running the store because he could keep up on all the gossip. I usually expected to see him and had remembered to get him a coffee from Red Truck Coffee because it was his favorite. "Hang on," I said, lifting a finger after we put the last box on a pallet, which was ready to be driven by forklift the short distance to the small store.

I leaned in between the plane seats and pulled out the untouched coffee. "Here you go," I said handing it over.

Stan put his palm over his heart in a gesture reminiscent of Diego. "Oh, man. I swear, that Cammi, she's an angel. Her coffee is straight from heaven, and I'm not even sure I believe in God."

I chuckled. "Not gonna argue with you on that. She just bought Misty Mountain Café too."

"Whoa," he said with a grin after he took a long swallow of his coffee. "She's going to be a monopoly. I wonder if her food is as good as her coffee."

I shrugged. "Not sure about that, but she told me she wanted to have breakfast leftover pizza, so I took that as a really good sign."

"That's freaking brilliant," Stan said. "Don't you know if she's a good cook? I thought you were seeing her."

Did I mention Stan was up on the gossip? Lord knows how this guy knew about me and Cammi. Although, Diamond Creek was a hub town in this part of Alaska. If anybody from this village was flying out, they went through Diamond Creek on the way. It was the main place for them to travel for any errands beyond the small offerings here in the village at the general store.

"How the hell do you know anything about who I'm dating?" I countered.

"I'm high-society, dude. Saw you at that fundraiser with her. Remember?"

"Oh shit, we did see you there. I meant to track you down to chat some more, but the night got away from me."

"Sure, the night got away from you. Better explanation was your eyes were stuck on Cammi. Now you listen," he said, his eyes lasering me as his gaze went somber. "She is a nice girl, and you better not screw her over. I heard about that bullshit that last guy pulled with her. Good thing I'm over here most of the time and not around to make a stink over there."

Of course, Stan would practically adopt Cammi. He was also that kind of guy. He loved people far and wide, which was how we became friends so quick when I took the job with Flynn. Stan had actually volunteered to fly with me and introduce me at some of the other villages.

I held both palms up in surrender. "Stan, I don't play games, and I wouldn't hurt Cammi."

He rolled his eyes. "I know that. I know you're a good guy and you're totally solid, but you're kind of, I don't know, a little mysterious, I think you got a past. So, I'm just saying don't let your baggage fuck with her."

I leaned my head back to stare at the sky as I took a deep breath. Was I that fucking obvious? Leveling my gaze with his again, I nodded. "I get it. I've got baggage. I'll do my best not to let it mess with her."

He nodded and cuffed me lightly on the shoulder. "Fair enough. We all got baggage. Lord knows, I do. I've had three wives, and now I'm back with my first one. Only took me..." He paused, counting on one hand. "...forty years to figure out I shoulda stayed with her to begin with."

I threw my head back with a hearty laugh. "Guess it's never too late to figure out the right thing to do, huh?"

"Damn straight. Now, I'm sure you're on a schedule, so you better get your ass in the air. I'll see you next time you're here for delivery, okay? Don't forget my coffee," he called as he strolled away and held the distinctive red cup up in the air.

Chapter Thirty

CAMMI

A few days later

I stared at my phone, rereading Elias's text for maybe the one-hundredth time. I didn't like admitting it to myself, but a teeny-tiny corner of my brain had been afraid there was some kind of a surprise waiting for me. There was no surprise. He wasn't the father. He'd told me he wasn't, but I'd still worried. I hated that I'd been so fucked up in my head about it.

I tapped out of that text and opened another, this one from Joel's soon to be ex-wife.

Hey, Cammi. I got your number from Joel's phone. He has no idea I'm texting you, and frankly I don't care if he finds out. I just wanted your number. I wanted you to know I officially filed for divorce, and I'm moving out of state with the kids. I also wanted to apologize once again. No matter what, remember, he betrayed you as much as me, and every other woman he's had affairs with. I'm not actually sure how many. You seem like a nice person, so I hope you don't let what happened with him mess with your head for too long. Trust me, hon, it's not worth it. You've got my number now, so if you ever need me, just call. I have no idea what I could do, but I'm all about good women being there for each other. Take care.

I shook my head slowly, my chest loosening up a little bit more every time I read her text.

Setting my phone down, I opened the folder of paint samples I'd picked up. The loan had closed, early as planned. Blessedly, none of the staff left, so Misty Mountain Café was running along without a hiccup. Susie was helping me get set up with a payroll system to take over the one they were already using. With the loan including fees to help with the transition, I was beyond relieved I could rely on a friend I trusted implicitly and also make sure she got paid.

Now, I wanted to get the place repainted before the summer tourism picked up too much. I was planning to do it in the evenings after we were closed, one wall at a time. I was deep into comparing paint samples when I heard a knock on the glass windows. Glancing over my shoulder, I saw my friends, Risa and Jessa, waving.

Setting down the samples, I crossed over to the door to unlock it and let them in. "What are you two doing here?"

Risa brushed her dark bangs away from her brown eyes, smiling as she replied, "We're here to have fun."

Jessa added, "Girls' night. We haven't had one in months. We figured we'd do it here if that's okay."

Risa managed Midnight Sun Arts Gallery, which was near the harbor. She was married to the local police chief, Darren Thomas, and also the sister of Trey Holden, Emma's husband. Jessa was one of the Hamilton's, the family who owned Last Frontier Lodge. She was married to Eli Brooks who ran an outdoor gear shop. Diamond Creek was always going to be a small town. Although I hadn't grown up with either one of them, they were both friends and part of the larger circle of women I knew well.

I had texted Risa earlier today asking for some feedback on colors. "I thought we could take a look at your paint ideas and then hang out," Risa explained.

"Sounds good to me," I replied. Anything to keep my mind off of what to do about Elias would work for me.

I threw the bolt on the door and gestured for them to come over to the counter. I had spread the samples over the counter in front of the espresso machine. Risa and Jessa immediately began looking through the samples. While Risa ran the gallery, Jessa herself was an artist. She sold whimsically painted furniture at the gallery here and others in Anchorage, in addition to San Francisco. She was fun and creative.

"I think go with one of these brighter options for an accent wall, maybe the plum, and then keep the other walls something neutral, either a soft gray, or cream. Something cream will be a little warmer for the space. Are you planning to keep artwork on the walls here?" Risa asked as she looked around.

Hands on hips, I nodded. "That was the other thing. I thought I could talk to you about potentially rotating art for sale through here."

Risa clapped her hands lightly. "That would be freaking perfect. I suggested that to the former owners, but they didn't want to have to worry about managing commissions. I think we can run all the payments through my gallery, and I give you a cut of the commission. How does that sound?"

"Freaking perfect," I said with a grin. Risa high-fived me. I turned to Jessa, adding, "We can always have a display of your furniture for one of the tables. It would be used, but it's a great way to display your work. What do you think?"

"Freaking perfect," Jessa parroted Risa and me.

We laughed together and then I brought my focus back to the color samples. "I think you're right on the accent wall. Maybe that's the one behind the register so the other walls are more neutral for displaying art."

"So, I've ordered pizza, and Emma is bringing the wine," Jessa explained. "Susie and Hannah will be here shortly, and Tess said she's on her way."

———

Within short order, our pizzas arrived, and Emma showed up with wine, declaring she'd offered to get it so she could vicariously enjoy it since she couldn't drink. She was looking awful ready to burst at this stage in her pregnancy.

Once we were all settled in and chatting, Tess asked, "So, did you have fun at the fundraiser?"

"It was great," I replied. "Your fundraisers always do well. Alaska is lucky to have you."

Tess had come to Alaska on vacation and fallen for Nathan while she was here. Although Alaska was much more spread out and sparsely populated, she did a bang-up job of managing fundraisers online and traveling to the larger communities.

"I didn't mean that," Tess said with a slight smile. "I meant did you have fun with Elias?"

It felt as if all of my friends rotated to look at me. I took a swallow of my water. I wasn't drinking because I needed to drive myself home.

"It's fine, but we're on a little hiatus while I get my shit together."

"What do you mean?" Tess pressed.

Emma immediately chimed in. "Let's not pressure her. We kind of have a crowd tonight."

"It's okay," I offered. "Long story short, I kind of had a meltdown after that thing with his ex-girlfriend showing up. It's fine. Turns out she needed him to do a paternity test, not because she thought he was the father of her son. It was because the actual father, his old friend who fooled around with her behind his back, died. His family was contesting her getting survivor benefits for their son. They claimed they thought Elias was the father."

"Oh, that sucks," Tess said.

Jessa reached over from where she sat beside me and squeezed my hand. "That's what we call all-caps awkward. But, what's the deal with you two?"

I took a bite of pizza before answering, "Well, I kind of flipped, thinking he was covering something up. And, we hadn't even really figured out what we were doing. It's not a shocker, but my baggage is recent and kind of heavy. I just told him I needed some time to get a grip."

"Have you gotten a grip?" Susie pressed.

I narrowed my eyes at her. "I'm working on it."

Susie opened her mouth to say more, but Emma cut in, "Pressure doesn't usually help anybody. It certainly didn't help you when you and Jared were trying to figure things out."

Susie had the grace to look sheepish and cast me a rueful smile. "Sorry. I'm just rooting for you two. It seems like he's pretty into you."

Conversation moved on to other matters, and the

group slowly broke apart a little while later. Emma lingered after the others left.

I was finishing up wiping down the table where we'd been gathered while she helped quietly. We were putting the towels in the laundry area behind the kitchen when she commented, "It'll take the time it takes for you, you know that, right?"

Glancing to her, I said, "I'm not sure what you mean."

"Figuring out when you're comfortable trusting yourself."

I felt as if I'd abruptly found the missing piece to a puzzle, but I wasn't sure where it went. "Trusting myself?" I prompted.

"Yeah. Trust isn't just about trusting someone else, it's about trusting ourselves to know when something feels right. My gut tells me you *do* trust Elias, but you're not so sure about you."

My chest hurt. There was a tight, pressing feeling, but when I took a breath it began to ease.

"It's hard to know when relationships start," she added.

"I don't even know if we were starting a relationship." I tossed the last towel in the bin for the load of laundry I would start in the morning. I was already developing a routine here. When I glanced her way, I saw her rub her lower back. "You need to sit down," I ordered.

Emma cast me a tired smile. "I've been sitting more than I prefer. I'm at that stage where nothing's too comfortable."

"Remind me when your due date is. It's soon, right?"

"May tenth, so I've still got a few weeks."

"You sure you don't need to sit down?" I prompted.

Emma nodded firmly. "Yes. Now, back to you." Much as I didn't really want to talk about Elias, I didn't mind because the last thing I wanted was to think too hard about how much I wished I could be pregnant and expecting a baby. I hated wishing for something so hard and feeling like it might never happen. I also wanted to focus on my joy for my friend, but it was hard not to think about babies when someone was expecting a baby.

If she noticed my internal tumult, Emma decided to ignore it. Her blue eyes held mine. "Maybe you weren't planning for a relationship, but it sure seems like that's what happened. Talk to him. You can trust yourself and still have people do shitty things. You did absolutely nothing wrong before. Joel or Brad, or whatever the hell his name was, lied to you about who he was. It's no good to go through life assuming everyone's going to do that. If there's one thing I can tell you, that's miserable."

Emma had gone through her own hell in an abusive relationship years ago. Even if I didn't know the intimate details, I knew she'd had to find her way through to the other side of it and come out whole.

"Let me ask you something." At my nod, she continued, "What would you tell a friend in the same situation?"

Another puzzle piece fell into place. "I mean, obviously I wouldn't blame them. I just can't believe I didn't realize he was lying." I faltered, wanting to explain more about all the reasons I couldn't trust myself, but Emma's steady gaze dissuaded me. It felt as if I were clinging to something that didn't make sense.

"Let's set aside the fact that you totally have the hots for Elias." Her lips twitched, and her eyes held a glint. "Would you tell a friend they could trust him?"

My head was nodding before I even thought about it. Because I knew without a doubt Elias was worthy of trust. Even when he used to be cranky with me, I knew he was a good man.

"Absolutely," I whispered.

Chapter Thirty-One

ELIAS

I had stopped to get coffee at Red Truck Coffee and was currently battling a sense of disappointment that Cammi wasn't here this morning. While she'd replied to my last text, I had heard nothing further.

I had things to tell her, and I was torn between respecting the space she'd asked for and not wanting to lose the opportunity to let her know how I felt. I was still grappling with how far and how fast I'd fallen for her. And yet, I supposed I'd been falling for her the entire time I was coming to her little coffee truck.

"Hey, Elias," a voice said over my shoulder.

Glancing back, I found Emma and Trey Holden. Trey was a fellow pilot, and Flynn had just bought out his single plane business, absorbing the plane, as well as his customers.

"How's it going, man?" Trey asked with a quick smile.

"Decent. I'm on my way out to fly. I've got a delivery run this morning and then a glacier view trip with some tourists this afternoon," I explained.

Emma smiled. "I'm so glad you guys bought his

plane. Now he's got more time to be home and not headed into an insanely busy summer."

"I'm sure you'll enjoy having the extra time," I commented to Trey. "Remind me when the baby's due."

Trey grinned. "May tenth."

"I'm hoping I beat that date," Emma offered with a light laugh.

Emma's pregnancy was what had prompted Trey to sell to begin with. He ran a small law practice as well. When he was doing that and flying, I imagined his schedule had been on overload in the summer.

"I hope it's early for you then," I said with a chuckle.

"Who's next?" Amy called.

I lifted my hand. "You know my order."

Amy cast me a sheepish smile. "Actually, Cammi's the one who's good at memorizing everyone's orders. I think I need a reminder."

"Don't feel bad," I replied. "That's a lot to remember." I quickly gave her my order and glanced over my shoulder. "I'll cover you two. Go ahead and tell her what you want."

"You sure? "Trey prompted.

"Absolutely. I'm gonna give her the money for your order anyway, so at least tell her."

Trey chuckled, just as Emma chimed in, "Just tea for me."

He finished their order, and we stepped to the side while Amy got our drinks ready.

A few minutes later, we were walking toward our trucks. Trey was parked right beside me. He was climbing in on the driver's side and the passenger door was facing my driver's door. Emma lightly caught my elbow just as I moved to open the door.

"Yeah?" I glanced to her.

"Cammi's painting Misty Mountain Café after hours."

"Oh?" I wasn't sure what to make of that.

She nodded. "She could use a little help."

Because I was a man and could be a little slow on the uptake sometimes, I asked, "Are you trying to tell me something?"

Emma sighed, and I heard Trey's low laugh from the driver's seat as she held the door open before she climbed in.

"Dude, she's obviously trying to tell you something," he called over.

Emma nodded firmly. "I'm definitely trying to tell you something. Good luck."

Bemused, I left and went to spend my day flying. That evening, I decided to take Emma's direct hint and aimed my truck toward Misty Mountain Café on the way home from work. When I pulled into the small parking lot in front of the coffee shop, the only vehicle there was Cammi's. She didn't have the outdoor lights on, but I could see her working through the windows. The entire front of the old Quonset hut that had been transformed into this coffee shop was windows. She was wearing a skirt and a T-shirt with tennis shoes as she stood on a ladder and carefully painted the upper edge of the wall behind the register.

I waited until she had lowered her arm because I didn't want to startle her and then knocked lightly on the door. She glanced over from the ladder, her eyes widening when she saw me there. She set the paint brush down and lifted her finger, indicating I should wait, before she slowly climbed down the ladder.

A minute later, she was opening the door, and my

heart was thudding so hard in my chest I thought it might crack a rib. Fuck, I had missed her.

She had a smear of paint on her cheek, and her hair was pulled back in what I thought was supposed to be a ponytail, except most of it was falling loose.

"Hey." Cammi's melodic voice spun around me with only one syllable.

"Hey."

I realized I was standing there like a fool when her brows hitched up in question. "Can I come in?" I asked.

"Of course." She stepped back, gesturing me through the door and closing and locking it behind me.

I scanned the space. It looked mostly like I recalled, but in all honesty, I always got my coffee at Red Truck Coffee, so I couldn't remember the last time I'd been in here. "Are you repainting the whole space?" I asked when my eyes made their way back to hers.

Cammi nodded, brushing a loose lock of hair away from her forehead with the back of her wrist. "One wall a night. I figure that's all I can get done at once."

We faced each other, and my pulse kept on humming while need tightened every fiber in my body. God, I wanted to kiss her.

"How does it feel to own this place now?" I forced myself to focus on anything but the feel of her lips underneath mine.

Her eyes did a quick arc around the café. When they landed back on me, she shrugged. "I'm not sure yet. I never expected this to happen, and now it's here."

"I missed you." I abruptly changed the subject

without planning on it. My feelings apparently decided they needed to be heard.

She looked at me quietly, and a sense of burgeoning filled the air. Her cheeks went a little pink and her lips kicked up at one corner. "I missed you too. I was going to call you."

Needing to make sure she knew I wasn't pressuring her, I added, "I wasn't saying that so you would. You can still have the space you need, but I was hoping I could let you know something."

She was quiet for several echoing beats of my heart, and I started to wonder if I was barreling forward to quickly. "Hey, I didn't mean—"

Cammi shook her head, and I quieted immediately. "I was just trying to figure out how to say what I wanted to say," she began. "I miss you. My freak out was more about not trusting myself than not trusting you. I know you're a good man, and I know you weren't hiding anything from me. I'm sorry I kind of..." She circled her hand in the air before dropping it. "Freaked out. It also kind of took me by surprise."

Joy was spinning inside the lust she always elicited. "I took you by surprise?"

"Well, you were all, you know, kind of grumpy and distant as long as I knew you. We never talked about what was happening, or what we were to each other. I didn't want to make any assumptions. Things happened fast, but then, I already knew you."

I took a step to close the distance between us, reaching for her hands. God, it felt good to touch her again, just to have that link of contact. "So that explains it. I already knew you."

"Yeah," she said slowly as if I was missing something. "What do you mean that explains it?"

"That explains why I fell in love with you. It didn't

happen that fast. It happened in slow-motion, and then my heart finally got the memo and caught up real quick."

Her cheeks went bright pink, and her mouth dropped open as her eyes went wide. "Do you, you—" she sputtered before she shook her head and snapped her mouth shut.

"I'm just telling you how I feel. Rumor has it I might've been a little slow on the ball with that. I know the whole thing with my ex-girlfriend—"

This time, it was Cammi who shook her head. She freed one of her hands from mine to place her finger over my lips. "You didn't do anything wrong with that. If I hadn't had such a weird, fucked up thing happen in my last relationship—if I can even call it that—I wouldn't have reacted the way I did. Is everything okay with that, by the way?"

She finally dropped her hand, and I immediately caught it in mine again as I nodded. "It's fine." If I had it my way, I'd never let her go. There was the inconvenient fact that life didn't make it possible for me to hold onto her *all* the time, but I would take what I could get.

Her pretty blue eyes searched mine and then she leaned up and pressed a kiss just under the edge of my jaw. When she pulled away, she said, "I guess I've been falling for you too and I just didn't know it." She swallowed and took a fast breath. "Actually, I love you."

My heart gave a rounding kick, and I moved to pull her closer, but she gave her head a little shake. "There's one more thing." Her brow creased, and she blinked a few times, looking suddenly nervous.

"What is it?"

"I want to have kids." Her words came out in a rush. She took a gulping breath. "A lot." Another pause and another deep breath. "I just need you to know that's really important to me. If you don't want kids, then you should tell me now."

Her eyes were bright, and she swallowed audibly. For a few seconds, I was startled. Not because she wanted kids, but because I suppose I hadn't expected to discuss it now. I took a breath and thought for a few seconds. The thing was I hadn't ever thought I'd fall for anyone again. But that was the *only* reason I hadn't thought about having kids. Before I'd let bitterness twine like a vine around my heart, I'd imagined having a family. The idea of that with Cammi? Well, that was easy.

I traced my knuckles along her jawline. "I haven't thought about it much, but that's only because I didn't expect to fall in love. If you really want kids, then I'm on board."

She stared at me—hard. I didn't realize she'd been holding her breath until it came out in a whoosh. When she tipped her forehead to rest on my chest, I finally wrapped her in my arms, in a full body clench. "I'm going to get paint on you," she murmured against my shoulder.

"Sweetheart, I've been flying and I'm probably filthy. I don't care about paint."

I loved the sound of her giggle. Of course, it was me, and Cammi was in my arms, so while I was trying to be romantic, my body had other ideas. Just when I was thinking I should step back to try to get some kind of a grip, I felt one of her hands slide up under the hem of my T-shirt. The feel of her palm on my skin set me on fire.

Another breath later, we were kissing, and I was taking deep sips from her warm, sweet mouth. We broke apart, breathless and laughing together.

I spun her around, lifting her and sliding her hips on the only clear space I could find on the counter. "Elias!" she gasped as I slid my palms up her silky thighs, letting her skirt bunch around her hips.

"What?" I dipped my head, trailing hot kisses along the side of her neck, satisfaction rolling through me when she arched into me and let out a little whimper.

"Somebody might see," she murmured when I lifted my head.

I brushed a wayward lock of hair off her cheek, letting my thumb trace her lips. I glanced over my shoulder. Looking back to her, I shook my head. "No, they can't. From the door, all anybody can see is that giant ladder and the sign blocking the view. We have to christen your new café," I coaxed.

Cammi's tongue darted out to glide across her bottom lip. She peered over my shoulder. "Okay, you better make it quick," she said with a sly grin.

"No problem with that. I don't think I can last long anyway. I missed you too much."

And then, I was pushing the damp silk out of the way between her thighs and tugging her hips closer to the edge of the counter. She made quick work of my fly, and I let out a rough growl at the feel of her silky palm curling around my shaft and sliding up and down in a teasing stroke.

"Hurry," she ordered.

I abruptly realized I did not have a condom. I came here with one plan, to tell Cammi how I felt. Shortsighted as I was, I hadn't realized I was going to get to show her with more than words.

I dropped my forehead to hers, pressing a fierce kiss to her lips. "Sweetheart, I don't have a condom. I wasn't really thinking ahead."

Her fingertips were pressing into the base of my spine, and she shifted her hips slightly. "I have an IUD. I promise I'm clean. After what happened before you, well, I got checked for everything."

I searched her eyes and pressed another kiss to her lips. "I'm only sure, if you are. I promise I'm clean."

"Hurry," she whispered fiercely, her eyes dark as they held mine.

I could work with any orders from her. I positioned my cock at her entrance and slid home in one deep thrust. My knees buckled. "Oh, Cammi," I slurred. Her satiny, clenching sheath felt beyond good, the pleasure indescribable.

With both of us half dressed, and her legs curled around my hips, we were chasing after our release together. I felt her channel rippling around me and reached between us to tease my fingers over her swollen clit. She cried out, and I followed her over the edge as my release whipsawed through me. I held her close while my thundering heartbeat gradually slowed.

After we hastily put our clothes back in place, Cammi took me on a quick tour and told me her plans. She then told me I had to go because she needed to finish painting her one wall for the night.

I didn't want to leave her side, not even a little, so I asked, "Why don't we paint the whole place tonight?"

Her eyes flew wide. "What? There's no way we can get that done."

I gestured around the space. "Sweetheart, there's four walls and the ceiling. You're not painting that, right?" Whoever had renovated this Quonset hut had put in an actual ceiling instead of the curved surface up top.

She nodded. "But—"

"You do the trim, and I'll follow behind on the walls. You already finished the trim on this wall right here. Between the two of us, I think we can have it done in a few hours."

I could see her chewing on the inside of her cheek as she looked around. "I'm game, because I get up early anyway. I can have one late night and then just be done with it. I feel like that's a lot to ask of you."

I shook my head, smiling as I pulled her into my arms again. "Nope. Either I sit here and watch you paint so I can go home with you, or we do it together. Might as well bust it out."

Chapter Thirty-Two

CAMMI

I stood with my hands on my hips as I spun in a small circle, looking around the coffee shop. It was done, completely painted, and it looked beautiful. I couldn't wait to hang the new artwork.

Elias was cleaning up in the storage area behind the kitchen. With one last look around, I hurried back there. He had all the paint brushes soaking in water and was closing up the last can of paint. I could tell he'd done some painting in his life. He had been remarkably efficient. We'd eventually switched so he could take care of the trim at the top of the ceilings while I did the bottom. It was quicker because he had better reach than I did.

"Thank you so much," I said, stopping in front of him. He tapped the can of paint closed with a rubber mallet and straightened. "Anytime, sweetheart. I'm good for projects."

I giggled as I reached for his free hand. "You are, huh?"

"Absolutely." His eyes flicked up to the clock on the wall. "It's not midnight yet. Let's go to bed."

Not much later, I fell asleep, tangled up in the sheets and held close against his muscled chest. I already knew his shoulder was the perfect place to tuck my head, but tonight, it felt different. For once, my mind wasn't spinning with questions and worry. I knew what my heart felt, and I trusted myself. Trusting him was the easy part.

EPILOGUE

Cammi

"Are you sure?"

Tess's curls bounced with her nod. "I am sure. You look incredible."

I turned sideways again, eyeing my growing belly in the mirror. I was having a shotgun wedding. Except no one had a shotgun. It's just that I was pregnant. Elias didn't want to wait anymore. I didn't either. It wasn't as if I'd been putting him off, but our lives had been incredibly busy.

With my expanded business situation, this year I'd felt like I was running a race every day. Thank goodness every night I got to fall asleep wrapped in Elias's arms. Once we found our way to each other, we hadn't wasted any time.

It became a running joke that he was spending the night at my place all the time, so I told him he should just move in. He did, only a month after we christened my new coffee shop.

Meanwhile, he was always flying while I worked like crazy, bouncing between my coffee truck and my new café. I loved our lives, because I knew he did too.

The only part I didn't love was when he had to do overnight trips. But that was life, and I would take it with all the blessings I had in abundance.

After I had my IUD removed, we thought it might take a little while to get pregnant. Apparently, in my case, my body was ready, or as Elias said, he had super sperm. Six weeks later, I was pregnant, and it turned out to be twins.

My wedding dress had had to be let out twice, and now I was worried it didn't look all that good.

"You look totally sexy," Susie said as she entered the room. "A pregnant bride is hot."

"Really?" I asked as I once again inspected my round belly in the mirror.

"Yes. You're in the perfect phase for this. You're pregnant enough to still be cute. You just wait. By nine months, you won't be feeling so hot, especially since you're having twins," Susie replied.

Hannah came into the room at that point and swatted Susie on the shoulder. "Really? No need to make her worry about it. Let her enjoy having an easy pregnancy."

Susie rolled her eyes dramatically and brushed a curl off her forehead. "She's already had an easy preg-nancy. She's not even having morning sickness."

Emma came in. "Out," she ordered. "It's time for the ceremony."

Emma was the best kind of friend. She was always a soothing presence just when I started to work myself into anxiety. In this case, I wasn't anxious about marrying Elias, it was more of the enormity of the moment because for a while, I hadn't thought I would find my person. I thought I might have to let go of my dream of having a family.

Only moments later, I was standing in front of

Elias. We weren't in a church. We were in the cathedral of nature. Although my parents weren't here to see the ceremony, we were having it in a field on their old property, which I'd been able to purchase with Elias only weeks after he moved in. Along with friends and family, we even invited the doctor who'd mistakenly thought I was Elias's girlfriend back when he was in the hospital. It seemed fitting.

The weather had cooperated beautifully. The sun was bright on this cool summer day, and there was only a little bit of an ocean breeze gusting through our small wedding party.

It honestly completely slipped my notice that anyone else was there. The moment Elias held my eyes and said "I do", I was lost in the moment and in his ebullient gaze.

ELIAS

Nora caught the bouquet of peonies, Cammi's favorite flower. The petals had fallen all over the place, because peonies were fragrant and a little messy, a lot like Cammi.

"What am I gonna do with these?" Nora said as she eyed them in her hand.

My sister, Faith, laughed. "I guess you're gonna fall in love."

Nora narrowed her eyes. "Fat chance of that. I don't believe in love." She and Gabriel's sort of secret on-again, off-again thing had been decidedly *off* lately.

Diego happened to be approaching at that moment and pressed his fist over his heart. "How can you say that? Love is a real thing. Do you believe in Elias and Cammi?"

Nora stared, kind of hard, at Diego. "Of course, I believe in Elias and Cammi. It's just love isn't for me. I don't think I have the right personality."

Diego rested his palm on her shoulder, giving it a light squeeze. "You'll know when it's right."

Nora glared at him, but I didn't dwell. It was my wedding day, and I had a girl to celebrate.

I sought Cammi out in the small crowd. We had our reception up at Last Frontier Lodge. There was enough space, and they refused to charge us, if only because we gave them so much business.

Cammi was chatting with my mother and Marley. I slipped my arm around her waist, unable to resist sliding my palm over the side of her round belly. She was fucking sexy as hell pregnant. Who knew I had a thing for pregnant women? To clarify, I didn't have a *thing* for anyone but Cammi. Cammi pregnant? Holy smokes. My body thought she was made of fire.

My mother smiled between us. Her health was doing better, and she had actually quit her job, which was a huge relief to me and my sisters. "I'm so happy for you two." She leaned up, cupping my cheek with her hand. "My boy was a little too cynical for a few years there." Her eyes shifted to Cammi when she dropped her hand. "You took him out of that place. I'm so grateful for you."

I felt Cammi's arm curl around my waist, and she squeezed lightly. "I consider myself the lucky one."

Two years later

.   .   .

A loud scream pierced the air. I was just coming through the front door, and my arms were laden with grocery bags. I braced myself. Sure enough, another scream followed and then the sound of two pairs of feet scurrying across the floor reached me. I smiled in spite of the chaos.

"Slow down!" Cammi called.

"No worries," I called in reply.

Only last month I had built an extra counter right by the kitchen door. Pretty much for the sole reason of dumping grocery bags by the door, although I told Cammi it was because she wanted a lower counter for baking. True story, but it was also handy.

I immediately unloaded the grocery bags just in time for the first twin to collide with my knees. Leaning down, I swung Eli up in the air, laughing as he giggled. I had this down to a science and set him on the floor just in time to catch Darla.

We knew Cammi was going to have twins, but we'd decided to wait on finding out the gender, only to be surprised with fraternal twins, a boy and a girl. Darla, who we named after Cammi's mother, came out two minutes earlier, so she was technically older and was already bossing her brother around at two.

"Daddy, daddy!" she called, immediately reaching for the one grocery bag that was hanging half off the counter.

I quickly nudged it out of her reach with my elbow. "Yes?"

"Did you get ice cream?" Eli chimed in.

"Maybe. You'll have to find out after dinner."

Cammi came walking in the kitchen then. She crossed the room, leaning up to press a kiss on the side of my neck. As she stepped back, I moved to slide my arm around her waist and reel her back in.

She came easily, laughing as she tucked her head against my shoulder, asking, "How was your day?"

"I spent most of the day in the air, so it was good. Yours?" I nuzzled her neck, breathing in her scent. "You smell like sugar," I murmured as I lifted my head.

"We made sugar cookies this morning," she said with a sheepish smile as she looked up at me. "It was kind of a disaster, but they taste good."

She gestured toward the stove, and I looked over to see a unique collection of shapes, all of them melted together into one giant cookie.

"Ah, sliced cookies," I said with a grin.

Our two-year old twins had already scampered back into the living room, which was conveniently through an archway so we could see what was going on. Twins were a handful and required almost constant supervision. There was the one bonus that they often kept each other occupied. Our house was entirely toddler proof, so for the most part we could steal a few minutes here and there.

I brushed Cammi's hair back from her face. "So, you had someone cover this afternoon?"

"Yes! With your mom taking the twins this afternoon, I took care of all my orders, and I could breathe."

Cammi was busy, all the time, with her coffee truck still in full swing from roughly March to November and the café year-round. With me flying, both of us were living at a breakneck pace, but it was a good chaos, and I wouldn't change it for a second. The twins made our life feel overflowing. We had to steal moments alone. That was okay too, because then it felt special. With my mother moving up here, we had some breathing room for daycare, plus plenty of friends who helped out.

"Too bad she didn't keep them for the night," I murmured as I leaned down to trail kisses along Cammi's neck. She giggled and arched into me before stepping back breathlessly. "Actually, she's picking them up again in twenty minutes."

"She is?"

Cammi stepped back just when I tried to kiss her again. "Yes. Remember? We have date night with Daphne and Flynn."

"I think we should cancel," I said flatly.

She cuffed me lightly on the shoulder. "No. We promised."

"Can we come home early?" I pressed.

I caught her hand and reeled her right back up against me. She was laughing as she looked up. "They're spending the night at your mom's house."

I stole a kiss while I could. Her eyes sparkled when she looked up at me as I drew away. "You're impatient."

"When it comes to you, always."

Thank you for reading Evers & Afters - I hope you loved Elias & Cammi's story!

Up next in the Dare With Me Series is Diego & Gemma's story.

Diego is *that* kind of hero - smokin' hot, deeply protective and with enough brawn to set the world on fire. Cue the melting.

He oozes the rugged hero vibe, rides a motorcycle and flies planes in the wilds of Alaska. He's *all* man and then some. When he meets Gemma, he falls fast, and she might be in need of a man to catch her when she falls.

Pre-order now! Come To Me

For more swoony & sassy romance...

This Crazy Love kicks off the Swoon Series - small town southern romance with enough heat to melt you! Jackson & Shay's story is epic - swoon-worthy & intensely emotional. Jackson just happens to be Shay's brother's best friend. He's also *seriously* easy on the eyes. Shay has a past, the kind of past she would most definitely like to forget. Past or not, Jackson is about to rock her world. Don't miss their story! Free on all retailers!

Burn For Me is a second chance romance for the ages. Sexy firefighters? Check. Rugged men? Check. Wrapped up together? Check. Brave the fire in this hot, small-town romance. Amelia & Cade were high school sweethearts & then it all fell apart. When they cross paths again, it's epic - don't miss Cade's story! Free on all retailers!

For more small town romance, take a visit to Last Frontier Lodge in Diamond Creek. A sexy, alpha SEAL meets his match with a brainy heroine in Take Me Home. Marley is all brains & Gage is all brawn. Sparks fly when their worlds collide. Don't miss Gage & Marley's story! Free on all retailers!

If sports romance lights your spark, check out The Play. Liam is a British footballer who falls for Olivia,

his doctor. A twist of forbidden heats up this swoon-
worthy & laugh-out-loud romance. Don't miss Liam &
Olivia's story.
Free on all retailers!

Sign up for my newsletter, so you can receive
information about upcoming new releases & receive a
FREE copy of one of my books: http://
jhcroixauthor.com/subscribe/

FIND MY BOOKS

Thank you for reading Evers & Afters! I hope you enjoyed the story. If so, you can help other readers find my books in a variety of ways.

1) Write a review!
2) Sign up for my newsletter, so you can receive information about upcoming new releases & receive a FREE copy of one of my books: http://jhcroixauthor.com/subscribe/
3) Like and follow my Amazon Author page at https://amazon.com/author/jhcroix
4) Follow me on Bookbub at https://www.bookbub.com/authors/j-h-croix
5) Follow me on Instagram at https://www.instagram.com/jhcroix/
6) Like my Facebook page at https://www.facebook.com/jhcroix

Dare With Me Series
Crash Into You
Evers & Afters
Come To Me - coming April 2021!
Back To Us - coming June 2021!
Swoon Series
This Crazy Love
Wait For Me
Break My Fall
Truly Madly Mine
Still Go Crazy
If We Dare
Steal My Heart
Into The Fire Series
Burn For Me
Slow Burn
Burn So Bad
Hot Mess
Burn So Good
Sweet Fire
Play With Fire
Melt With You
Burn For You
Crash & Burn
That Snowy Night
Brit Boys Sports Romance
The Play
Big Win
Out Of Bounds
Play Me
Naughty Wish
Diamond Creek Alaska Novels
When Love Comes
Follow Love
Love Unbroken

Love Untamed
Tumble Into Love
Christmas Nights
Last Frontier Lodge Novels
Take Me Home
Love at Last
Just This Once
Falling Fast
Stay With Me
When We Fall
Hold Me Close
Crazy For You
Just Us

ACKNOWLEDGMENTS

Every story I write starts with one character in my imagination. In this case, Cammi has been skipping through my thoughts since my first published book where she appeared as a side character. Readers have emailed me asking when she'd get her story, and I kept saying something along the lines of: someday, I promise!

I was starting to worry because Cammi's hero wasn't showing up for me. Then, Elias strolled into Flynn & Daphne's story, and I knew he was Cammi's hero on the very first page he appeared. To all the readers who asked about her story: thank you for your patience!

Gracious thanks to my editor and to Terri D. Many thanks to my early readers and to the bloggers who spread the word about my stories. Extra thanks to the early readers who happen to be detail queens as well.

So many thanks to my assistant, Erin, who makes my job so much easier and helps me focus on my stories.

ACKNOWLEDGMENTS

Every story I write starts with one character in my imagination. In this case, Cammi has been skipping through my thoughts since my first published book where she appeared as a side character. Readers have emailed me asking when she'd get her story, and I kept saying something along the lines of: someday, I promise!

I was starting to worry because Cammi's hero wasn't showing up for me. Then, Elias strolled into Flynn & Daphne's story, and I knew he was Cammi's hero on the very first page he appeared. To all the readers who asked about her story: thank you for your patience!

Gracious thanks to my editor and to Terri D. Many thanks to my early readers and to the bloggers who spread the word about my stories. Extra thanks to the early readers who happen to be detail queens as well.

So many thanks to my assistant, Erin, who makes my job so much easier and helps me focus on my stories.

Every book makes it to the finish line with my dogs keeping me company and with my husband cheering me on.

xoxo
  J.H. Croix

ABOUT THE AUTHOR

USA Today Bestselling Author J. H. Croix lives in a
small town in the historical farmlands of Maine with
her husband and two spoiled dogs. Croix writes
contemporary romance with sassy women and alpha
men who aren't afraid to show some emotion. Her
love for quirky small-towns and the characters that
inhabit them shines through in her writing. Take a
walk on the wild side of romance with her bestselling
novels!

Places you can find me:
jhcroixauthor.com
jhcroix@jhcroix.com

facebook.com/jhcroix
instagram.com/jhcroix
bookbub.com/authors/j-h-croix

Made in the USA
Coppell, TX
07 May 2021